praise for
suicidemusic

suicidemusic

suicidemusic

paul jessup

Editing and Interior Formatting by Katherine Silva
Cover Art & Design by Luke Spooner | Carrion House Illustration

ISBN (Paperback):
ISBN (Digital online):
First paperback edition: July 2025
First digital edition: July 2025
Published by Third Estate Books
https://www.thirdestatebooks.com

For Liam
Here is a story of hope

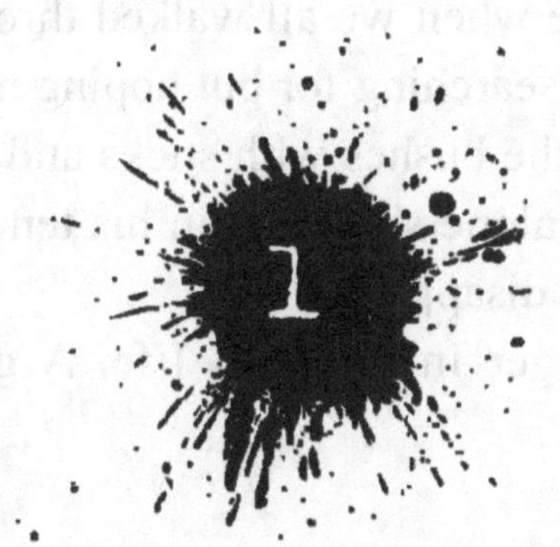

I want to forget my skin. My skin is not who I am. I want to close my eyes and let my breath burn me alive from the inside out. The world doesn't feel right; everything feels wrong. I want my skin to go slack and fly away, toss and breathe discarded in that summer breeze. Everything has changed. Everything is different now. These memories held inside my skin… I want to break free from all of them. I want to change. I want to cease to be me.

Can I take off my skin now? Can I become a ghost? I can't deal with this.

Oh god no.

They...they found my brother Casper yesterday out by the pines. Just a crumpled body unmoving, unable to move, all skin and bones. They carried him like an infant back to the ambulance. I wasn't there, but the image was everywhere. A picture snapped. Stick frail brother boy with oxygen mask over his face, his hair in clumps on his head and the hunter who found him carrying him with big strong arms over to the stretcher. That picture. It spread across the internet and magazine covers. Everyone in the world saw it. It was a beacon of sorts. Missing teenager found.

Everyone had an opinion. Comment sections lit up, social media feeds created hashtag storms. None of them knew anything at all. Just the void shouting at the void.

They weren't there when we all walked through the woods with the cops and the dogs searching for but hoping not to find his body. I was there. I beat into the bushes with sticks and called out his name, and then spent nights alone shivering in his tent. Waiting maybe for the rapture or my own disappearance.

I felt like a stranger in my own life. A ghost without form, without sound.

I remember him being found: Mom dropping the phone. The look on her face wasn't the face I've come to know over the years. Gone were the stern lines and edges, now replaced with panic, fear, and terror. She picked up the phone with shaking hands, and sought shelter behind the line of tents to a place where she thought I couldn't hear her. Her words became a wave of whispers crashing along my ears. I tried to hear. I tried to eavesdrop. But I couldn't make out the words no matter how hard I tried.

Eventually the call ended and she came back. There were tears on her cheeks and her body had tiny tremors, like little earthquakes erupting in her blood. "They finally...they finally found him. Oh fuck. They...they found him. Come on, let's go. We need to go. We need to go to the hospital. Right? Yes. Right. That's right. They found him, Hazel. Come on, come on, Hazel, let's go. They found him."

And before I could grab a few things and get ready, she collapsed. I ran forward, tried to hold her body but I was all dizzy myself. I pushed her upright, her drooping head on my shoulder blade. "I'm sorry," she said, "I just… I don't know."

"I can drive." My voice was stronger than I ever knew possible.

"Right." Hers was distant; distinct, "Just don't. Don't let them pull you over. Just a permit."

"Let's go. He needs us, come on. Just forget all of that and let's go."

She seems so small suddenly. We're almost the exact same height but she seemed so frail in that moment. Not like a mom, like a child. And for once? For once, I was terrified of the future.

We got into the car. We drove to the hospital.

I'm next to his body. It feels strange to stand here and hold his hand. Cold hand so cold hand. It's frail, too. I don't want to touch it. It feels like I can break it. Will I break it? I look over at his face. The oxygen mask distorts his features. His hair is thin in parts and tufts in others. Red holes surround around his eyes and mom says that's where someone had sewed them shut. The doctors removed the thread earlier. I'm glad I wasn't here for that.

"Read to him," Mom says, "He likes that and I can't... Not right now. It feels...too much. I feel too much." She turns her head so I can't see her cry. "Just like when he was little and I read to him. Just listening and attentive."

"Okay," I say. My voice is hoarse but it's going to have to do. A soft amber glow of small lights dots along the ceiling. Low light. Like electronic candle light. The doctors say it's better for him somehow. I don't know how. Somehow. "What's a good book?"

Mom takes a careless finger to a stack next to the bed. "One of these... Some of these... Something like that, I guess."

A mix of children's books flat and hard boarded, and underneath are longer works. Intellectual works with thousands of pages and complex translations. I try to think of which to read. Which would be better for me? Which would be better for him?

I pull out some large, long book from a writer unknown to me. The cover looks foreboding and literary and the title is a single word (Sleepless) and it feels somehow oddly fitting. I turn to the first page, hesitant to start reading. I look over at mom. "Okay? Is this okay?"

She is full of lightning. "No. Nothing's okay."

"Oh. Okay."

"Just read."

And I do.

"Come on, you should go back to the site and get some sleep."

Dylan's leaning against the brick wall and smoking as he talks.

He looks like a ripped up ramshackle tent propped up against the wind. His body about ready to collapse in on itself. "It's not like your brother's just going to pop up wide awake like a jack-in-the-box while you're gone. And I'm sure your mom will call you if he does." He looks me over, stares at my body piece by piece as if he wants to touch each part, even though we're not together anymore. "You need to go back. Come on."

I'm digging my nails into my arm and I'm thinking of cutting myself again. I don't want to do that. It's been years since I did that last and I don't want to do it. In my mind, the blade is against my arm, and yeah, it hurts for a moment. But the hurt isn't the point. The way it feels after the hurt…that's it. The release of something inside, something building up and boiling over. I want to cut it out. I need to cut it out.

"Hey, what's going on? You here with me? Come on, Hazel." He grabs my shoulder and I move back away from his fingers.

"Stop it. You don't get to touch me right now."

"Okay. Yeah. Okay. Sorry. I'm just saying we should go back, right?"

"Fuck you, Dylan."

"All right then. I'm sorry, I know shit's tense between us and all, but I came here to help. You need help, don't you? Just go back to the site, sleep in your tent for a night and get some rest. It will all be okay."

I walk past him. I want to kick him in the face. I want to dig my blood out with knives. "It won't be okay. What makes you think I want to go back there? What makes you say that? It's not home. None of that is home. Don't you get that?"

"Well. This isn't home either."

"Get out of my face. Go and piss off someone else."

"Yeah. Okay. Fine. All right. I'm going to go back to the campground and guard your guy's shit until you can get back, okay?"

I turn and walk back through the double glass doors.

"Whatever."

That campsite. Fuck that place. I didn't want to live there anyway. None of us did. It was just an act of survival. You live in a small town and the factory shuts down? There aren't any shelters. There's no place for you to go but into the woods. I hate that place. I never thought I would miss the Safe House before, but I do now. Mom can't afford it, insurance won't cover it, but it was warm and I had friends. Close friends, friends who went through the same stuff I went through. But that was behind me now, I guess. Now we live out here, in the campsite, far away from the lives we used to live.

Right after we went there, my brother ended up missing and now look what happened. I smelled like smoke every day at school. Not like cigarette shit, but like firewood. Like burning up. I smelled like fire fire fire...

Maybe that's it. Maybe I need to burn up, burn alive. Maybe then I'll get this shit out of me, get it out from under my skin. Maybe if I light my skin up, I would be a ghost, and then all this bad blood and bones and flesh would be gone.

When something like this happens, everybody seems to come out and show support. It's a strange feeling. Everyone telling you awkward private things, like that your brother is an inspiration to them. Or that they'll pray for you, or that you're in their thoughts. I know they mean well, but what does it really mean? What does any of it mean? Are the words just empty things? More voids feeling the need to shout words into the night? Everywhere I see emptiness behind the mask of human compassion. Do they feel like they have to?

Still, I nod and say thank you. I want to get the awkwardness over as quickly as possible.

The book's closed on my lap and Mom's asleep on two plastic chairs pushed together. I feel bad not reading, but reading doesn't seem to do much of anything for him. All of the machines make the same machine noises. Nothing seems to change. Everything feels empty right now. I think of turning on the tv, but then what?

What to watch? Would the sound of it give him bad dreams? Will he dream of late-night reruns? I try and picture how Cheers would appear in a coma nightmare and decide that no one needs that.

I see a text from Clara.

How you holding up?

I'm not sure how to respond to this.

Okay. I guess.

It doesn't take long for her to respond.

Bullshit. I'm coming over.

Coming over? This isn't a slumber party.

You can't. Visiting hours are over.

I don't want her to come over. I don't want friends right now. I just want my brother back. I want everything back to normal.

I think of all those scalpels they have hidden around here, and how I want to use them to dig these feelings out from inside of me.

Meet me outside. I'll be there in 5. My mom is freaking me out. I just need to get out of here. She's not making sense.

Huh. Knowing Clara, she won't take no for an answer. I look over at Mom. She looks like Mom again: curled up and dreaming, no longer like some lost child looking for a parent. I look over at Casper, my brother, and I see everything is stable and nothing is changing at all.

I guess it will be okay. I get up and go.

"Come on, you'll like this. It's a good surprise, I promise," Clara said.

We're running through the back alleys, light and conversation filtering down from cracked-open windows. A parking lot opens up in front of us, all concrete and emptiness, with the old school behind it.

"I don't know. I just...I feel like I'm abandoning him right now. What if he wakes up?"

Clara didn't even stop; she kept running as she called out behind. "Hurray! Then he wakes up, we run back to the hospital and it's all happy times."

"Happy times?"

"Yeah. You going to be sad if he wakes up? Whatever happens, you'll be happy to see him again. Come on. Get over it. Let's have some fun."

"Fun. Yeah. Okay."

As we dart across the empty parking lot, Clara pulls a cheap-ass jug of wine out of her coat. That nasty tasting juice box wine with a screw on cap that always gave me the worst hangovers in the morning. But for some reason, Clara just loves that shit. She waves it in the air and hoots. "Come on! Fun!"

And I laugh. Clara definitely knows how to cheer me up. We run to the old school glancing around to see if we spot someone drifting by that would get us in trouble. Sure, it's late, but you never knew. You get a bored cop or a drunk asshole and the whole thing would go sour really quick. And I need this right now. Maybe Clara did too.

The school itself is large, brick and rotting. The windows are boarded up, and spray-painted sigils cover random parts like drunk spells cast in early occult hours. We peek around, then she pulls out bolt cutters, and snips the old chain lock. We slip inside into the shadows and the shaky foundations.

We move through the debris, climbing over fallen chunks of concrete, pushing through veils of spiderwebs like ghost hands on our faces. The graffiti looks like something holy with moonbeams drifting down through ceiling cracks, and I pause and look at them. I'm tempted to pull out my phone and take a few pictures, but that feels wrong somehow. Like making this permanent would destroy the moment.

Clara practically shoves the jug in my face and I take a nip. It's a heavy big thing and the wine tastes like alcoholic Kool-Aid. I almost spit it out.

"Fuck, that's disgusting!"

She laughs. "Okay, princess. What did you expect? A nice pinot noir and maybe some caviar?"

I hand the jug back to her. "Oh, shut it," and then look at the graffiti a little longer. It's complicated. It's intricate. For spray paint, it seems impressive, like a human body, but dissected in a way that looks religious. I want to touch it. I think about touching it.

"Come on," Clara says, "We need to get to a safe spot."

"Safe spot?"

"Yeah. Come on, drinking and urban exploration don't mix, you know?"

"Oh, right. Then why did you suggest it?"

"Because it's fun. It wouldn't be as much fun if it weren't so dangerous now, would it?"

"I guess not."

I turn away from the mural. It looks like it's shifting out of the corner of my eye, the blood pumping through spray painted ventricles. Something moves under my skin again, moves inside of my blood, banging on my bones to get out and get free… I ignore it for now. Drinking will shut it up. Drinking always does.

The safe spot isn't safe. But still, we drink. We perch in the remains of the garden.

"You know, I used to have a thing. For your brother, right?"

"No, I didn't know that." Laughter. "Do you want to have a coma wedding now?"

"Oh, fuck you. I never said the w-word."

"Right, but he's my big bro-bro. I can't have you breaking his heart. Have to make a respectable woman out of him."

She laughs and it's almost a chortle and not a chortle at the same time. "Shut it. I'm just saying, right? Just saying he's like...I don't know. It hurts to look at him now."

"You haven't seen him though."

"Yeah, I have. Like, online and stuff. All those pictures of his rescue."

The thing inside of me starts digging through me, starts screaming and howling. It's an animal--I realize that now. It's a wild thing wanting to claw itself out of me. I want to scream and scream and scream. Screaming isn't always a good thing. "That's not the same thing. Those are...pictures. Lenses and mirrors. Those are...distortions. Not real."

"You're not real."

"Shut it."

"I'm trying to say...I don't know. What can we do?"

And then I'm quiet. All of me is quiet. Every part of me is quiet. My hair and blood and lungs and everything. My skin is slack against my bones and I pull my knees up to my chest. I don't want to talk about this anymore. What can we do?

I take a gulp from the jug and it burns my everything and sends tingles through my body. I want to be nothing. I want to black out and burn up and cease to exist. I shake my head, cough, and say, "I don't know."

She pauses for a moment, let's me know she's serious before she talks. "Well. Let's make a list."

"Fuck you."

"I'm serious. Let's itemize our possibilities. We can't bring him back, right? But what if we figured out what happened to him? I mean, wouldn't that help?"

I hand the jug back to her outstretched hand. "I guess. In what way?"

She swigs, then speaks. "Because if we find out what happened to him, then maybe they can figure out how to fix him, right?"

"Maybe. I don't know."

"Come on. Let's go all girl detective on the situation. Besides, it can't hurt?"

I take another swig. It's a stupid idea. I know it's a bad thought. I know it's asking for us to get hurt somehow. To go missing ourselves. But the cops aren't doing anything, are they? And the doctors are stumbling in the dark. Maybe this won't help them, but maybe it could help me.

I look at my trembling hands. They shake like my mom's the night they called. I think it might help me. It might make me feel like something other than *this*.

"Okay," I say and think maybe this will keep me from cutting myself open.

We wake up to the sun in the ruins of a garden. The taste of chalk is in my mouth. I don't know why I taste chalk, but I do, and I feel like I had tiny insects crawling all over me in the night.

Clara is in the old white tree in the center of the garden, trying not to fall as she rolls herself awake. The leaves are dead and they cling to her hair and face.

"You hungry?" she calls down.

My head is exploding and I crave coffee.

"I guess. Maybe? I think I need caffeine more than anything."

I watch her climb down the bones of the tree. Her body moves like ballet and I wish I could be that graceful. I know I'm a klutz. All my limbs feel too big for my body.

"Let's get some coffee then," she says, "I've got a few bucks. Maybe some toast or something too? I dunno. Let's just get out of here. This place is boring in the daylight. Like it lost all of the ghosts."

I look around and think it still looks beautiful in the early morning light, even hung over and fuzzy headed. Clara had a ghost thing though. She preferred the midnight hours: reading Poe and holding séances. I tried to tell her that stuff was kind of hokey, but that would make her sad.

"Okay. Yeah. I could use something in my stomach other than nasty wine."

We climb out, careful, careful, out towards the daylight.

"Okay. So. Clues."

Clara's got a crayon that came with the child's menu in her hand. She's writing on a stack of loose napkins. Between us are scattered plates covered in toast crumbs and pieces of egg. Coffee sits in front of me; water to my left. "Clues," I say.

"Like, give me some clues."

I look at her like she's insane.

"Come on, I can't do this all by myself! Fine, give me a second to Google a few things."

She looks up some stuff on her phone and I try to think of what she could mean by "clues." All I can think of is my brother in that hospital bed, his face still and his eyes covered in red holes from the stitches they removed earlier. The doctors walking around his body like he was dead already, their eyes betraying what they knew, that they knew he would be dead even if he woke up. He would be a ghost in that body, haunting it with the past. I feel emptiness behind everything.

I see the faces around me and feel like they hide a chasm, a black hole of being. Masks that are made of bone and eyes and hair and teeth.

"Okay," Clara says, "Like this: I have a map of where they found him. That's a good place to start, right? Oh…and this is interesting. Did you know that Dylan was the last person who saw him? Before he went missing? Another clue. I need to write these down."

I nod. I feel like everything is further and further away. Did Clara just say something about Dylan? It felt important, but all I can think about was when they found my brother, how they found him. I'm spiraling through shadows, and I need to stop. "They sewed his eyes shut."

Clara doesn't say anything.

I feel like falling and the light is so different. I want to go see him now. I need to see him right now. And I want to explode right then and there, I want to take whatever was inside of me and let it out, let it free. I couldn't keep doing this, every day, every day, how could I keep doing this every day? I want to be free of all this. And I can't help it; I have to shove these thoughts down inside. It's what I've always done, it's the only way to survive in this world. If I let it out and they saw, really saw what was going on inside of me? That would be the end of everything. So, I shove it down, and say as calmly as I could I say, "That's a clue, right?"

And Clara looks at me, and I just hope Clara doesn't notice my mask slipping.

"Come on, let's go back to my house for a little. I think you need that."

She's paying for the bill with piles of quarters and crumpled dollar bills.

"No, I think. I think I need to see him. I need to make sure he's still real, you know?"

I feel like crying and decide against it. It's not easy, the tears fight against my eyes but Clara doesn't need to see this, any of it. This is mine. This is personal. This pain is not her pain.

"Okay. I guess."

She says these words like she doesn't mean them. I look at her and wonder why she is so hell bent on being around me right now. Why she wants to play detective so badly. I then look into her eyes and I see fear curled up and lonesome. Fear of the future, fear of the present, an overwhelming fear of everything. And that's when I realize why she's doing this detective thing. She needs control over something.

Everything is out of control.

I can understand that.

"We can do more later, okay?"

"Okay."

She finishes paying and we walk towards the front of the diner. All the people here are like old strangers, ghosts of themselves looking for what they lost years ago. The emptiness is still there behind their faces staring at me. They seem angry that I figured out their secret. They want to destroy me for it.

We go outside and she says, "Can I? Can I see him? Not long… Like a second or something." Her words struggle for air.

"Yeah." I look at my feet. "Okay."

Dylan's waiting at the double glass doors in front of the hospital. His eyes are sleepless. His face seems pinched tight and hungry for violence. "There you are," he says, sturdy like a building, "You had me worried."

Clara looks at him and at me. "I thought you two..."

"We did. Move, Dylan."

I think about pushing him aside, but that would make him happy on some level: to feel my touch. That just creeps me out even more, like I'm covered in shadows.

"I went to the site, like I said, and made sure no one stole your stuff."

"Congrats," I say, "You want a cookie? Move aside. I want to see my fucking brother already, you asshole."

"Please, just...please. Clara? Can you talk some sense into her? The poets wanted to get to the campsite, and I was making sure that they would stay away. He's targeting you, you know. The Poet is coming for you. Tell her, Clara! Tell her."

Clara does an exaggerated cartoon shrug and I try not to laugh.

Dylan's face is scarlet. After a second of clenching every muscle in his body, he lets out a long sigh like it was trapped in his lungs forever and his whole body goes slack like an old school zombie, head bowed and body ready to shuffle off in search of living food.

"Look. I just… I wanted…to keep you safe. Okay? I need to keep you safe. It's not what you think, okay? I need to keep them away from you the best I can. I just wanted you to say 'thanks.' Why can't I have a 'thank you?' That's all. I'm trying to keep them from turning you into poem, and you can't even say thank you once!"

Clara moves forward a little. "Hazel needs to see her brother. Can't you see that? Please let us through so she can do that."

Dylan moves aside, deflated.

As we walk past, his eyes seem hungry and frightened, like a dog lost in the wilderness.

"Keep me safe from what?"

His head snaps up with a ratcheting cracking sound. His fingers move in the air like they're living things, spiders hanging down from delicate webs, hunting something. But what? I feel closed in, and need to run. What the hell did I ever see in this guy?

He creeps forward, moving like a shadow moves across concrete. His face is twisted up, like he sees something terrifying, just out of the corner of his eyes. "The Poet is targeting you, don't you see?. The birds: they listen for him, for them, the poets, for Clara's mom." His gaze is intense, eyes bugging out, biting on his lower lips, twitching. "Shhhh. We can't do this now." Finger to his lips. "Shhhh. They're going to start doing things more and more and more. It will all ramp up and their art will be everywhere. They will make everything into…"

And he pauses and the look of terror is complete on his face. Pure abject horror, unlike anything I've seen in real life, and it gives me goosebumps and I want to scream and run away. He then whispers this last word, haunting in the air. "Poetry."

We watch as he grabs a bird mid-flight by the entrance and with a quick snip, kills it in his fingers. "Shhh, there you go. You won't go and talk to anyone now, will you? A secret… A secret between you and me. Going to go now. Going to keep us safe now."

He leaves, almost running out into the parking lot with the dead bird in his hand.

We don't move; we can't move. Stunned silence is the only reaction to something like this happening.

Clara reaches out, grabs my hand instinctively. Part of me, still shook up, wants to shrug her off, to shrink from her touch. But instead, we stand there in mute silence for a moment, holding hands, unable to move, unable to speak.

Eventually Clara breaks the silence. "Fuck that, come on, let's go." And she pulls me inside the hospital and I realize, yes, we have something we need to do after all. I need to see him. She needs to see him. We need to make sure my brother's still somewhat okay. Well, as okay as he's going to be, all things considered.

Mom leaves the minute we walk in the room. She wants to run downstairs for breakfast and maybe a coffee. The panic in her eyes lets me know that she needs more than just food or comfort. She needs to be out of the room. She needs to have a moment where this isn't happening.

I understand. We let her go, and she doesn't even really give Clara a second glance.

"Just. Um. You know, call or something if he changes," Mom says.

I don't respond. How do you answer that? Yes, okay, yeah, affirmative… They all seem like the wrong words. Instead, I nod. A silent agreement that works well enough for the two of us.

After she's gone, Clara walks up to my brother. She touches his hand and almost jumps back. "He feels so..."

I move to the chair by the window. The sun is coming in. I see dust motes scatter as I sit, and feel like I'm in a painting. "…Fragile." I say.

She studies the oxygen mask over his face, at what's left of his hair and at the scars around his eyes. She touches a cheek gently.

I know how she feels. But I can't watch this. I turn and look out the window at the rows and rows of cars. They look like toys all lined up. A rainbow of colors.

"I can't believe..." She's crying.

I know what she means. "It's like he's barely even here anymore."

"What the hell? I mean. What the hell. Why did he bring up my mom?" Clara's shaking, her whole body tense and vibrating. Her eyes twitch, and I can't tell if it's anger or fear or what. Tears, and maybe it's sadness?

I don't know. I feel so numb, like even my bones are floating. I could float away and I want Clara to anchor me, but she can't. She's floating away, too.

"Hazel? How is this right? How is this okay? He's so fragile now. He's all bones and like...did they starve him? Did they? Why would anyone do something like this at all? I don't understand." She puts her face into her hands. Her emotions are alien here. These are my emotions, not hers, and how dare she feel them.

And I want to cut myself again. I want to turn myself inside out. I need to be free. I need to get rid of this body. I need to set myself on fire. I need to do something. I need to do anything.

"What's to understand?" I ask. I'm numb. I can't take this all in. Why can't I encapsulate the world? Why can't everything be inside of me where I can fix all of it.

"Nothing, I guess," Clara says, lifting her head up from her hands, tears streaking her face.

"Right."

"When do you think your mom's going to be back?"

I don't know, so I don't answer.

There is a bird outside of the window beating against it, trying to get in. I've never seen a bird like this before. It's kind of like a robin? But not somehow. The red is too red and its eyes don't look right. Its beak is poised in a screech.

I feel everything in the air grow tighter. Like it's being pulled tight by tiny strings.

The bird beats harder and harder against the window. Feathers fly up and smash against it. I think maybe I should open it? But then what? Then what would the bird do in here?

I look over at my brother and the machine still beeping in rhythm. Everything seems fine for him. Clara's not even paying attention to the bird. It's like I'm the only one who sees it.

The bird smashes again. Harder. Harder… As if it's trying to break the glass.

Eventually it falls.

Sometimes my brother mumbles and his eyes dart about under his eyelids.

This gives us hope.

After my mom comes back, we each take turns trying to call Dad. He's been gone for over two years now. He won't ever answer the phone. When he left, he told us he would keep in touch and everything. That never happened. Nothing ever happened.

We try and email and we text. He has to know, doesn't he? It's been all over the place: online, offline, all of that. He doesn't answer or anything at all. It's like he doesn't care. Why doesn't he care?

Fuck him. It's his son. It's his family. Why did he do this to us?

Fuck him. I don't care. I don't want to care. He's a phantom limb, just itching and never really there when anyone needs him.

Mom's crying and Clara's holding her. Even though Clara's not really ours, she's become one of the family over the years. Oddly enough, I'm thankful she's here right now. I can't handle all of this by myself. I have enough things trying to break free from my skin without having to take care of my mom, too.

"You guys can always, you know, crash with us?" Clara says. "My mom said it's okay. If you need a break from the hospital."

My mom doesn't respond, but I know her answer will be no. It's always no. She doesn't want to be that kind of person. She doesn't want to be a burden. She already feels so lost and useless now, I can tell by looking at her. She can't find work anymore, no one can. Not in this town where everything is closed and the only jobs are replaced by automated tellers at the supermarket. It's all SNAP and whatever we can beg. We scrape by as best we can. And now this. I don't even want to consider what the hospital bill is going to cost. I hate that I think about those things. But sometimes it's easier than thinking about my brother: a ghost in a hospital bed.

"Maybe tonight," I say and my mom buries her head into Clara's chest. "Just me tonight, you know. Like a slumber party."

My mom lets out a scream and I know the way that scream tastes. I've had that same scream locked up inside of me for so long. I hope that soon I can let it out before it devours me.

I'm down in the cafeteria. It's late now. It's going to close soon and I wanted to grab something to eat. It's different than the school cafeteria, yet somehow it's the same. There's coffee here, and the food is half-priced since they'll be throwing it all out soon enough. I grab some granola bars, and a few bits of chocolate. I'm not really hungry but I feel like maybe eating might help? I don't know.

Clara's already got some food and is sitting at a table waiting for me. She has this heavy look on her face. I know that look. I think I might have it all the time now. That feeling of defeat, of everything being on fire. The whole world is a burning house. You run around trying to save everything, but you can't.

"I hate feeling like this. I know I should be hungry; I've barely eaten anything today." Clara stares at her food. "When I look at this food I feel like everything around me is tasteless. If that makes sense?"

I nod in agreement.

"You okay?"

I laugh. "What a stupid question. Of course I'm not okay. What about you? You okay?"

"Oh. I guess not. So, you're sure you want to come with me tonight?"

"I guess."

"You know it will help, even if only a little bit."

I look at the steak knife I picked up while grabbing peanuts. I don't have steak or anything thick. But I felt like I needed the knife. I think about pocketing it, and maybe cutting later. Not much, nothing visible. Just a little to let that blood out into the air and maybe get some peace.

"What do you want to do? Tonight, I mean. I have movies and stuff. Board games. Anything, you know? To try and get your mind off of things."

"Sure. I guess."

I can't help it. I can't think about anything other than my blood burning in my veins and my heart… My heart is a wild animal. My heart wants to maul me. My heart is a bear. My heart is a hungry bear. And I'm going to cut it out. I'm going to *bleed* it out.

That's when clarity hits. I grab Clara's hand with mine. I look at her, really look at her. I know what we need to do now. We can't keep running and trying to avoid reality. We needed to barrel forward like a rocket. "Let's do it."

She looks scared. "Let's do what?"

"Let's go and play detective. Let's try and fix this shit before it gets worse. Get out your scattered napkins full of clues and let's get sleuthing."

We're in the graveyard. Clara's electric lamp rests on the ground between us. The cold blue light fights with the night, carving shadows out of the tombstones. Owls hoot and we can hear them swooping to catch mice. It feels like something out of a bad horror movie from the seventies. That's probably why Clara brought us here. She was always one for a kick ass aesthetic.

Clara clears her throat and pulls up the pile of napkins.

"Okay, one: Dylan was the last person who saw Casper. I was able to get a hacker friend of mine to get into the police database and snag a transcript of the police interviews with him after your brother disappeared, but it's just gibberish. Like Dylan was rambling and it made no sense.

"Two: we know where he was found: out by the pines and about an hour from your campsite. Three: he was hanging out with Rowan and his weird crew almost non-stop the week before."

I'm quiet. There isn't much we could do this late, right? Maybe. It doesn't feel like real action, not yet. I need to ease into it. Danger clings to this whole operation. But I have to do it. I can't leave my brother there and do nothing. Will this wake him up? Probably not. But it is something. I have to do something.

"Let me read the transcript."

"It's nonsense. He sounded completely nuts."

"Just let me read it. It might have clues? Like, hidden in the nonsense."

"We can't keep going over what he said. It's a dead end: trust me on that. We need to gather more clues, get more evidence."

I pause. She's right. Enough inaction. It was terrifying to take that first step, but we had to take it.

"What do you suggest?"

"Well, we have two possible eye witnesses of sorts. Dylan, or Rowan and his crew. We could talk to Dylan ourselves, and maybe get a clearer response than the police. Ask him to explain somethings."

Our eyes meet like steel across the night, my anger seething behind my gaze. Fucking Dylan. Fuck him. I don't mind reading what he said to the cops, but I definitely do not want to see him again, let alone talk to him in person.

Clara reads my expression. "Rowan it is."

"It's midnight. What the hell? How do you plan on doing this? Break into his parents' house and drag him out for a middle of the night interview?"

Clara pushes her hair behind her ears and smiles. The smile makes me feel unsettled. "I have connections, Hazel, my dear. I have connections."

"You ever dream of the end of the world? You know. Like everyone is dead. That kind of thing.

"Once or twice, I dreamt that everyone fell asleep and the lake rose up and swallowed everything. I remember waking up when I saw all of these still, sleeping bodies on the lake bottom, hair moving around their heads like underwater hair, their eyes closed.. Kind of weird now that I think about it. I was dreaming about the world dreaming."

We find Rowan in an old industrial complex. The windows are smashed in, and he sits cross-legged on a ruined table. Around him flock some followers, people I know from school. Mostly popular kids, preppies in their letterman jackets toting pompoms. Now, they were dressed down and unwashed, like they'd lived in a cave for months, never seeing the light of day or bathing.

Rowan watches with interested eyes as we crawl through the debris. Hanging from the ceiling and bursting from the ground are countless rusting machines. Blades cover them. Gears stick out of them. Vines crawl over them.

He's in the back. An old office of sorts. Maybe for the foreman? The giant glass window is broken. Rocks poke out with circular cracks bursting around them. He doesn't move from his perch, even though his friends mill about. They pass shadow shapes from one to the other. Smoke waves up and then stops and we hear ragged coughing.

I look over at Clara. "Okay, girl detective, you got a plan?"

She smiles a crooked thin-lip smile. "Nope. Let's rock."

"Leave us be for a bit. I think we need some alone time for what's going to pass," Rowan announces.

His friends don't even grumble. They move all at once: their body machines slick and well-oiled move like clockwork. After they leave, Rowan nods and motions for us to sit. "Come on," he says, "Relax a little bit."

Clara and I stand. Sitting feels like it would put him on a pedestal. We need the leverage of height. The way he looks at us seems like he's trying to control us. His cold gray eyes. His thick lips. His mess of curly black hair. Sit. Sit. Sit. We don't sit and he seems slightly disappointed, but also curious.

"I hear your brother's back. That's good."

I nod. I don't want to talk. His eyes make me feel like I'm full of night, like everything inside of me is gone and darkness remains. Maybe coming here was a bad idea. Maybe we should've snooped and looked for clues elsewhere.

Doors slam shut like a gunshot in the dark. I can't help but ask. "What was that?"

"Nothing. They're going out, picking up a few small things." He pauses, runs his hands through his hair, turns his intense eyes at me.

I really want to punch him, or cut myself, or both. Somehow, blood will flow. Mine, his, whatever. I resist this urge as he continues on.

"What do you think of my place? It's like a Lynchian dream, don't you think? Practically poetic in its architecture, like a muse for the madness inside of me. Whenever I have a block and all those words are trapped in my head, I just need to look around. Everything springs to life. Everything is full of death. Your brother...he helped pick this place out. That was before he lost the light of the sun. Back when he still understood the voice of the Poet, understood the tragedy of his last poem. His daughter."

I want to be more subtle, but Clara jumps right in with a line of questions. "What did you guys do, you know? Before Casper left? Hazel told me he kept going out at night and not coming back until way late."

His eyes were fireworks. "Poetry."

Clara laughed, so hard she almost fell over. "Poetry?"

I don't believe it either, it sounded so silly. "I didn't think Casper was, um, you know, the poetic type."

I try to remember my brother as he was before. And I try to picture him writing poetry. The brother boy who was flunking out of English. The brother who once set a copy of Notes from the Underground on fire because he hated reading it.

Rowan crawls forward, towards us, on hands and knees, his eyes wide and his smile shining brightly. He looks manic, unstable like an atom ready to explode. "Oh yes, poetry, poetry! That wave of words that bursts out from our lips like the lake overflowing. Boom! Anarchy in form and context! We drown everyone with the sound and fury of our art. Poetry, yes. Poetry. Taught to us all by the master Poet, the one who sacrificed the most. His own blood, spilled to create his magnum opus, his masterpiece."

We both share a hesitant, confused glance. Clara coughs out a nervous "Okay..."

"No, it's cool. You probably think we got fucked up or something. I mean, that's what everyone thinks, right? Not that we don't get fucked up. Poetry requires a certain frame of mind...a way of peering behind what is physical and real in front of us and seeing beyond it. You ever read Plato?"

He's crawling towards us now, slip slow, on the ground. Moving like a snake on his belly, wriggling, his hands in the air, making shadows across the walls. I reach over and grab Clara's hand, palm to sweaty palm. I can feel her shaking, nervous, a bit scared. We both are, and it's hard not to be scared right now. His shadow puppets feel alive in an unsettling way. How could his hands make those shapes?

"Plato, yeah. Never mind. Just kind of like, poetry as transubstantiation, right? It's like, we become something more real. Like, this whole reality thing is a shadow and poetry can burst it wide open." He rolls over, springs up on the balls of his feet, his hair wild and covering his face. Only his eyes peek out, like two bloodied moons in a sea of hair. His fingers explode, expand and contract with each word. "Boom, boom, boom! We are the exposed hearts! Boom, boom, boom! We are the wild birds let loose from our skulls. You get me? Of course you don't. I can see it in your eyes. You're not a poet. You could never kill anyone."

And now he smiles, all teeth grinding, spittle flinging out of his mouth at that last sentence. His fingers are covered in dirt and I wonder if it's grave dirt.

Clara steps back and I have to hold her still. These are answers, even if they aren't the answers to our question, somehow they're connected. Somehow they're all related to what happened to my brother, what happened to Casper. Fuck.

Clara tugs again, trying to get out of here, away from danger. But I keep her anchored and say, "What are you even talking about? Killing people? What are you trying to imply--"

He holds up his hands, silence. Palms are covered in crisp new tattoos of open eyes. "Metaphorically speaking... Come on. Keep up with me. I'm talking about poetry, right? Poetry. The sun guides us, brings us closer to the entrance of the cave." He then closes his hands, pushes his long fingernails into his palms. Blood drips down, drip, drip, striking a rhythm to his words. "Sometimes you need to tear out your own eyes to see it, you know? Sometimes that's what the sun requires."

Clara looks at me and I look back at her and I feel an electrical current in the air. She has the same look I have—*fear, run run run, fear.* There is something wrong in the air. I think of my brother with his eyes stitched shut. If she tried to leave now, I would follow her. The answers here make no sense, and the danger is too great. Rowan seems poised, like a serpent ready to strike. "What the hell are you talking about?"

"It's all words, right? Nothing but words scattered around the earth." He uncoils his spine. "Come on, why you girls looking so tense? It's just us poets right now. That's all! And poets are completely harmless. Want something to drink? Want a smoke? Want to get fucked up?" His smile seems even sharper than before. Luring us in, trying to think everything is normal. But nothing is normal here.

"Not really," Clara says, and grips my hand even tighter.

"Smart then, right? Smart. Like Persephone or some shit. It's like you're pulling on poetry and you don't even know it! Bam! See it? See it everywhere? Poetry." His face is completely covered by his hair, not even his eyes shining out anymore, not even his teeth. It's so unnerving. To know his face is in there, somewhere, watching us, hungrily, with the eyes of a hunter.

I nod, try to appear calm and cool and collected, even though everything inside of me is a live-wire. It's not just the way he moves, it's what he sees. It gets under my skin in a way I can't explain. Clara squeezes my fingers even further, and I say, "Speaking of poetry, I was, um… I was wondering if you have any of my brother's poetry with you? I was thinking it might help us reach him in his coma."

Rowan crouches back down on the balls of his feet. "No, no I don't have anything for him. And 'cause you asked, and 'cause I'm a gentlemen like that, I'll answer the implied question." A smile appears then, in the shadows. Glinting teeth all bright and sharp. He rubs his hands together, the blood smearing across his palms. "We used to have readings. Got it? Me and these gang of wild poets would get together here and perform all night." He leaps up to his full height and rubs his palms against his face. Blood smears like sharp red slashes against his cheeks, tangles and mats his hair. His eyes are wild, bloodshot. "People would come from an hour or two away just to hear us. I even put some of that shit up on YouTube. You got it? There. That was it."

He laughs, then: a slow, soft laughter that boils in his chest. It stings to hear it, like salt poured in a wound. "Now get the fuck out of here before the others get back. I thought you had the poetry inside of you, but it's gone." He holds up his bloody hands in front of him, the eye tattoos smeared with blood, blinding them. "You're just as blind as the rest of them. You wouldn't see the sun if it was exploding in your fucking face!"

He lunges forward, and I stumble back in shock, almost falling on Clara.

"Get out! Get out! Get the fuck out!" His blood and spittle splash us with each word.

We don't wait around. We run, past the cracked window and all the ominous broken machinery. We stumble and almost fall, hand in hand. Everything is moving to my heartbeat, I feel my temples throb, my leg muscles tighten and beads of sweat roll down the back of my neck, fear overtaking everything, everything, when…

Clara pulls away from me. I feel lost and adrift as she says, "Cheese!" and snaps a pic on her phone. Her hands shaking as she did it, I saw a primal animal fear in her eyes, yet she was still strong, still present, still defiant against her own fright.

Rowan steps backward for a moment, his head tilted at an angle, his hair bloodied and whipping about his features. He runs a hand through his hair, and snaps his fingers and points at us. "I had a dream I was a crimson butterfly, laying my larva in the head of dead children. There, there you go. A parting gift from me to you, a poem inspired by the muse of this moment."

Clara puts her phone away. I'm still frozen now, the moment encasing me, sealing my fate. She grabs my hand, says, "Come on, we need to get going, come on!"

"Why did you do that?" I half-whisper.

Clara walks a little faster, pulling me onward, as Rowan grins behind us in the dark. "I thought it would piss him off. He deserves to be pissed off."

We're back at Clara's house now. Her mom is asleep, and she's laying out sleeping bags on the floor. They're covered in tiny skull prints. Popcorn pops in the microwave; the smell is overpowering and artificial.

"You know my house is haunted?" she asks as she puts her head down on her pillow.

I look at her. "Yeah? I didn't know that."

"When I was a kid, I did a séance here with my dolls and stuff. One of them started talking, and it was, like, the ghost of this woman. She lost her life in a fire. This house was built on the ashes of her house. That's why she haunts it."

"Oh. That's pretty creepy?"

"Naw." The microwave dings and Clara sits up. "She's nice. I like her. I'm just telling you so you don't get freaked out in the middle of the night. You know, if ghost stuff starts happening. It's all cool. Especially if you smell smoke, or the house looks like it's on fire. That's her, that's all. That's just her."

And then she leans in, whispers closely. "She keeps me safe from my mom, and the Poet, and his daughter."

I wake up in the middle of the night to the smell of wood burning. I don't know if it's me I smell or if it's the ghost. Am I even real? Have I become a ghost?

I remember my dream. A tree covered in dead snakes. A slow drum beat. Movement in the shadows pulling me closer. Pulling me nearer. I didn't want that tree. Something about that tree… It stays in my mind, and I want to go towards it as if it was a real thing and not a dream thing. I want to live in that tree, hanging from the branches like the dead.

Clara sits at a table in her kitchen, tired. The chairs are plastic and covered in tacky flower prints. Morning light beams through a glass door behind her that leads out to trees and a garden. Her mom built that garden from the ground up, messy and puzzled. The light reminds me of childhood summers but I don't want to think about that.

Coffee is on the table. Coffee for me.

"Did you hear?"

I sit down silently.

"Last night. I mean. Did you check the news this morning?"

"No." I pick up the coffee. Something feels wrong. The air feels wrong. It's like this bad feeling followed us from the factory last night, Rowan's wicked spirit haunting the air. I couldn't shake it, a feel of oppressive doom.

"Fifteen. While we slept. *Fifteen*."

"Fifteen?"

"More people went missing from our high school."

"Oh."

We don't say anything. I don't want to look this up. I don't want to go online this morning. I know all the social networks will be buzzing. Armchair detectives slinging conspiracy theories. I don't need all that buzz right now. I need to be solid and I don't feel solid. I feel like I'm existing between two worlds, like everything is permeable. Like my fingers can push through the air and reach over to the other side. Which side am I on? Which is the real world? Which is the dream? I think I'm the dream. I'm made out of dreams, built out of airy things like light, like smoke.

"People we know?"

"Probably? Though they're not releasing any names yet."

"Oh."

The table between us is spotless. No crumbs, no piles of papers. It exists as the perfect clean thing, like everything in this house. I am surrounded by clean. This clean will suffocate me.

What is this place? Who is Clara? Who are her parents? I can't ask these things. I have to get out. I have to get away.

"Hazel, listen…" She moves a hand across the table and gently grabs mine, connecting us. The touch is a shock and I want to run, but I stay. "We need to go further into this. We need to find out what happened."

I pull my hand back, hold it to my chest and look down. I don't feel tethered to anything. I'm floating, I'm indistinct. I'm a ghost. I'm not me anymore. "I don't know, Clara... I don't know. What will happen if we do? I feel like this is dangerous. We're being dangerous now."

"We need to. Hazel. Hazel, see me, look at me, please. We need to do this."

I look at my best friend and see all this clean surrounding her. All this perfection of upper middle-class existence. It's like she's living in a sitcom. I see her as she really is. How she will never truly understand me. She lives in a shell, in a bubble. Her problems are so small, so minor, that she needs to build problems to solve.

My problems are my problems. They are big enough to swallow the world. Homelessness. Brother in a coma. Dad missing and uncaring. Mom turning into a child. These are my problems. I don't need to create new ones.

"Why? Why do we..."

Clara's eyes are big and sad. "Because we have to stop this."

I look out to the garden. I think there is a fire in that garden, one we can't see, one that lives in the light. That fire is all light and the real that we see is the smoke, the shadow cast. The wild animal is inside of me again, turning and moving and dancing under my bones. I want to cut the wild animal of my heart out again and be free of this horrible feeling. I want to scream.

"I had a dream last night." I say. "I dreamt of a tree covered in dead snakes. I dreamt of a slow drum pounding. I saw a little girl in the center of that tree, encased in crystal."

Clara dry heaves. Runs to the bathroom. I hear her vomiting.

I remember when we were younger. Casper had found out that you could climb the tree out of our bedroom window and get on the roof. This was back when we had a house and a dad. When we had all those suburban Disney dreams that construct the American psychosis. We climbed up, higher, up to the tiles that scattered across the house. There was tar and stuff and it was hot to the touch. We looked up towards the sky.

I remember him looking out over the city. We were pretty little. And he said, "Hey watch. This is all just shadows of a fire," and he ran and leapt off the roof with his arms outstretched.

Birds scattered out of his way, and he floated for a while. His body was beautiful against the sky-scape. The whole town was beneath his body and I thought I wanted to join him. I wanted to do this. But I was frightened. I was too scared to run. I was too scared to jump.

So, I just watched him. Watched him float over the city to the lake. Watched his body pierce clouds and sun. Watched as he become more real then, more physical in the sky than on earth. Maybe he was a poet after all, and I couldn't really see it.

All the missing people had the same dream the night before they disappeared. A dream of the dead snake tree and the slow drum beat.

Car ride to the hospital. Clara's mom is driving us. It's a minivan, of course. Would her mom drive anything else? It's full of organic snacks for Clara. Clara's an only child. You could see that her mom wants to adopt all these lost teenagers that hang around in Clara's circle. I don't need that. I don't need some surrogate suburban family.

I'm quiet. Clara is quiet. Her mom is chatty.

"How's your brother doing? Is he doing better? The Poet's been asking about him again."

I don't say anything.

"Oh, that's too bad. I pray for him, you know? Pray every day. I even sent a prayer chain to my church group via email. Isn't that wonderful? All those people praying for him. He's bound to get better soon. What with all that positive energy. Prayer is a little like poetry, isn't it? It's a poem that is also a spell, a whisper between you and the universe."

She looks at me in the rear-view mirror. The smile she gives makes me feel like the world is collapsing. She looks like she wants me to say something? I don't know what to say to this.

"It's okay, you don't have to say thank you. I know you mean it."

The rest of the car ride is quiet. When she smiles in the rearview mirror, it feels wrong and broken.

Nothing's changed. I hoped that maybe when I got back today everything would be better. My brother would be sitting up. Maybe talking, maybe not. Maybe reading, maybe not. Mom would be smiling. Everything would be good. But. No. He's still there, the ghost of him still far away from his body. I was hoping that maybe it would be a trade? Like, the people who went missing would be a trade in for him, and then he would be okay.

I know it's wrong to think this. But I thought it and I wanted it to be true. I wanted my brother back. I wanted everything to be normal again. Maybe then, I will feel real. Maybe then, I won't feel like a ghost. Maybe then this creature inside of me will be quiet. Maybe then, I won't feel the desire to cut myself open, to let the air take my blood away.

Mom's standing against the wall outside of his hospital room. Her eyes are closed. Her whole body is leaning like the wall is propping her up and she can't hold herself upright anymore.

I say, "Mom," and my voice is so small I don't even recognize it. My voice floats away from me. It's become a voice of the air, like a voice made of ether, constructed out of the past trying to force its way into the present. A scratchy old record voice. My voice is becoming a memory and everything is constructed out of pieces of the past.

She doesn't open her eyes as she says, "I don't know if we can keep doing this... Can we keep doing this?"

"Yes." I hug her. She practically collapses in my arms.

"I need him back; I need him here. Oh, my little boy, my little man..."

She doesn't feel like my mom in that moment. She feels like a stranger and I disconnect with everything. Am I even Hazel anymore? Everything feels different.

Clara went with her mom to go do suburban family things, like shop for groceries at Whole Foods or something like that. She said she would call me later. I'm not sure if I'm going to answer when she does. I feel like somehow Clara isn't a real friend? Because her life and my life are two different spheres. She can't get it no matter how hard she tries. But maybe it doesn't matter. Maybe it's not important for her to get it? Still, I feel so alone when I'm with her.

I need friends. Or maybe I don't. I don't know right now. I don't know anything right now.

Straps tie my brother's wrists and ankles to the hospital bed. I guess Mom said he had this…fit. Punching the air. Tearing the tubes out of his skin. Screaming and yelling and trying to claw his eyes out of his head. I can see the marks on his face. Deep marks. He wasn't playing around.

But he's not moving now. He's muttering sleep sounds. "Doorways," he says. "Doorways."

I touch his arm and he doesn't respond. Mom is outside for a bit. She said she needed to get out of the hospital to breathe. I get it. She wants to be here for him, but being here for him means so much. It hurts me so much. Every time I look at him, I want to cut myself. It makes me want to grab knives and just let go, let the thing inside of me come out through my blood, strong and invincible.

Should I tell him? I wish I knew what he'd dreamt the day before he went missing. Was it the same dream I'd had? Was it a different dream? I need to know.

"I saw it," I say, not knowing what to expect, "I saw the dead snake tree in my dreams."

And he laughs. He's still asleep. He's still in a coma. But he laughs a sleep laugh and it sounds like something out of a movie. Something distant and far away. This laugh isn't right. It isn't real. It's small and broken and it makes me move back away from him.

The wild animal inside of me starts banging against my bones again. I want to let it all out. I want to scream. I want to bleed. I don't want this thing inside of me anymore. I want to be free.

Mom's back in Casper's room and I had to step outside. Everything feels wrong, like reality is wearing the wrong skin, and I'm waiting for the world to undress in front of me, to show me the growling heart beneath. Maybe I'm going crazy? I don't know. I touch the tree out by the parking lot. It feels real. I walk over to the cars, hot in the sun. I walk over to the front of the hospital. It's a long path winding about and scattered with stones.

The front is under construction. Workers yell at each other from suspended girders. People walk through the front door. Someone limps. One person holds his arm and has this ready-to-scream look on his face. Another runs in. I wonder why they're going through the front, and not through the ER doors out back. Unless maybe they're getting tests?

Families walk past, filtering on through. A haggard mom sits on a bench and smokes cigarette after cigarette, all the while surrounded by little girls all the same age, each wearing little bird masks. I feel like I'm haunted by little bird girls. The mom looks like she's about to panic, and snuffs her smoke out on the sole of her shoe. She tells the little girls to go in, come on, go inside, leave the nice workers alone.

I remember what Dylan did to that bird and I want to warn them. I'm about to warn them, when one runs up to me, looking secretive, like she's about to tell me something precious and private. Her bird mask bobs when she runs. She motions me to lean down and I do and then she whispers into my ear, "They are taking the heads off. They are filling them with tiny poems."

And then she runs off. Sparks fly overhead. Someone laughs and fog starts to roll in, roll up, take over and obscure everything. I want to get lost in the fog. I think about disappearing into it. Becoming fog. Becoming dream.

I am mist. I am vaporized water droplets. I am the ground-cloud.

I'm standing there while the doors slowly close. "Get the fuck out. Get the fuck away from me."

Dylan's walks up to the elevator. He leans forward, forces his hands inside as the doors slide back.

I shove him.

He moves back and the doors start closing again.

"I don't want anything to do with you anymore. Why can't you leave me the fuck alone?"

He doesn't say anything. He runs forward, crams his whole body through the doors as they close.

I think I should scream. I should just open up my lungs and let it out. I feel so claustrophobic in this small space. This little box without light, without sun, without anything.

He's sweating. He pants for a second. Hands on knees. Looks at me. "Fuck. What the fuck? What's wrong with you?"

"Go away."

He looks hurt but I don't care. My words are the only weapons I have.

"Look. Damnit. Look. My sister...she's... Fuck. She's gone okay? She's gone. She's one of the fifteen that went missing last night... and...fuck. The window was open, and there were muddy footprints all over the floor."

"Why...why are you telling me this?"

His hair is a mess. His hands have dirt on them. His nails are bent, broken. I can see cuts and burns all over his fingers. I can't help but see him as a culprit and not a victim.

I want to press a button. Move this elevator up or down or open the doors. I want him to go away. I want to curl up into nothing.

"Because. You know… Your brother."

"Get out."

"I can't. I can't even get out of my own head."

"What do you want me to do?"

He looks up at me. His face is fractured, full of conflicting emotions.

I hope for the doors to open. For someone to open this elevator up. To shine light into our little box.

"I know."

"You know what?"

He shakes his head.

I remember when we first started dating all those long months ago. I thought he was smart, brilliant, could talk for hours on existentialism. I thought that was hot, that his big brain was super sexy. But after a while the cracks started to show. His intellect was a sham. His big brain was tidbits cobbled together from Wikipedia articles. He's never read anything much longer than a tweet or a Facebook post. And now I see him here: I see the cardboard him in front of me, trying to be something he's not. I fear him, I pity him, I want to burn him alive. He is nothing. Was he ever anything?

"You and Clara went to talk to Rowan last night. You were asking questions, right? I know you're investigating or something. I want to help. I need to help. She's...she's all alone out there? You know? I remember, oh damn. She is scared of thunder. I used to yell at the sky to make her laugh when the thunder came. I used to fight the lightning, just for her. We need to get them back, before..."

"Before what?"

He looks at the ground. He can't meet my eyes. His mouth mumbles words.

"Before she ends up like your brother."

That was it. "Get the fuck out of here. Now."

The elevator doors seem to open on their own and he goes, he *goes*.

I spend a minute sitting on the ground as the elevator rises up to my brother's floor. I've got my arms wrapped around my knees and over the speakers, I hear static in the form of music. It seems like music made of empty sounds. I think about the dream I had, I think about all those missing friends. I think of my brother, my mother, myself. I think of my dream.

I feel like I'm falling and it's like in *Alice in Wonderland*, where she's floating down the hole, floating through the world into the land beneath lands. I float up, she floats down, we all float in a circle. I want to stand, but I feel like standing would light me up and I would be like an angel over everything.

I pinch myself. It hurts. But does that mean I'm real? Does that mean I'm a dream? I feel nothing inside of me now. The urge to cut is quiet. The urge to burn alive is quiet. The creature under my ribs wearing my heart as a mask is quiet.

I am nothing anymore. I never thought I would miss that feeling: exploding from the outside in, but I do now, because that feeling was something. It was part of me. Now? Now. I am nothing now. I feel nothing now. I feel like that fog outside. Just mist, draining the world of colors and shapes. Living only general outlines, basic shadows. Leaving nothing.

The elevator doors open and I can't move.

I just...

Sit.

They stand open and I roll my head on my shoulders.

Eventually they close again and I remain. Waiting for everything to stop. Waiting for the world to end. Waiting for the doors to open again. Close again. Waiting for anything, for everything. I am always waiting. I wait to become. I wait to exist. I wait to dream myself into being. I wait. I wait. The doors open again and all I see is a group of nurses huddled together and talking and laughing. They are lit by the hallway lights and they don't even see me.

Do I exist?

The door closes.
It opens again.
I have no answers anymore.

Eventually I move. Eventually I gather the strength to do it. All of me is heavy. I move slowly. I move like fog rolling. Nothing feels familiar to me anymore. I feel lost in these hallways. I feel like I don't know anything. Where am I? Was this the wrong floor?

I wander in the flickering shadows down some vacant passages and hear people praying. I look in and see them sitting over some child who was bald and sitting still and on fire. Every part of him was on fire: golden fire that lashes out from his skin. I watch them pray and I don't understand what language this is. I don't understand anything.

I walk away and then see this is the right place, the right floor, the right hallways. Mom stands outside of the room. She doesn't see me. She doesn't know I'm here. I'm a ghost floating by as she's punching the wall. She's hitting it and screaming and I see blood on her fists, on her head, too, and I wonder why, why? Oh my god, Mom. Oh my god, what have you done?

I'm floating in slow motion up to her. She still doesn't see me. I touch her shoulder. Now, I am real. Now, I am physical. Now, I exist.

She turns and looks at me. There are no tears, only lightning under her skin.

"Why won't he wake up? Why is this? Why? I can't. I can't. I can't. I try and I can't. I try and it won't change. I read and I show pictures and I talk and I talk. They say he's not brain dead, right? The MRI's all say he's fine, he's only sleeping and someday he'll wake up again and it will all be okay. But it's not okay! It won't be okay! Hazel, oh, why? Why won't he *wake the fuck up already?*"

I don't speak. She doesn't need my words right now. I know this. I just hug her and she trembles in my arms.

"You need to get out of there."

Clara's called me and I have no idea if we can still be friends anymore or not. I'm still so numb.

"No. It's okay. I just… My brother needs me here."

"That's your mom talking, isn't it? Be a rebel teen. Come on. Get out and come with me."

"I just..."

"Nothing. You just nothing. I'll be there in two minutes. Mom's letting me snag her car, and we have some shit to do."

"We do?"

The tree. The dead snake tree. The tree. It's in my skull now.

"Yes, we do. We're going to save some missing kids and it will feel *awesome*."

"Who will save me?"

"What?"

"Nothing. Five minutes?"

"Yup."

"I'll go outside."

Clara's driving. To the left and right are pines. The road is roughshod, and it bumps as we ride along it. The pines move like something is jumping from tree to tree, from branch to branch. The music on the stereo sounds more like static to me. The road ahead is engulfed in fog and I feel like I'm in an episode of old school *Scooby-Doo*. Any minute now, some creepy thing will shamble out of the woods and erupt in an insane laugh.

Clara is talking again. I don't know. This car smells like Febreze and I just want the moon to fall from the sky.

"Anyway, so. Yeah," Clara breaks the silence.

"Yeah?"

"Yeah."

"That email."

"Oh, right! I forget to fill you in on the detail. This morning, I got an email and it's weird because the email address is like gibberish and it doesn't exist. They probably spoofed the header or something hacky like that. Anyway, it had, like, a video attachment? And it was showing the area where there was that midway or whatever, from when we were kids, with all the rides."

"The one that closed down a few years ago?"

"That's the one. It's in ruins now. Amazing how fast nature takes over once everyone is gone. Anyway, while the camera or drone is moving around and showing the place, in the background there's...I don't know. Wait a minute."

She reaches into her bag and keeps steering as she pulls her phone out. Keeping an eye on the road and an eye on the phone, she clicks through some stuff then hands it to me. "Here," she says, "Watch it."

Shaky shots of the lake, of birds, of the pines nearby. I know the place. The small rides are covered in moss and mold and rust. The souvenir booths are hollow shells. The drone keeps going down the midway, down to the arcade that was old when I was a kid. There, the camera floats through old machines and then I hear it. I hear what she's talking about.

Cries of help and hunger. The sound of metal scraping on metal. Everything inside of me is now electrified, like I'm being shocked back awake. Goosebumps cover my skin. And behind that? Behind it all? The sounds of someone whispering poetry. Barely audible, but there it was, the broken verse of a modernist poem.

These stones that were her eyes, yes
And these hands, that grasp and crawl across the floor

"Holy shit."

"Yeah. See?"

"What the fuck, Clara? Why didn't you just send me this? I would have come running."

"Well, we're going now, right?"

"Right, I guess."

"Okay."

"Why did they send it to you?"

"Dunno."

"Did you send it to the cops?"

Clara doesn't say anything. We drive a little further, and—yeah—I know she didn't send it to the cops. I know that without her even saying it once. The cops are all bumbling and fumbling. Some of them even feel dangerous, like wolves dressed up and standing as policeman with big teeth and guns. Either way, they won't help. They won't solve anything. Ever.

I remember: me and my brother, both of us smaller and younger. Running through the midway. Running through the park. I think it was called Falling Lights or something like that. I remember big neon, blinking signs everywhere. The smell of elephant ears and corndogs. Kids running and screaming. Adults laughing and drinking beer from plastic cups.

My brother played in the arcade. Non-stop all the time. He didn't even like going on rides. What a weirdo. He plunked quarters into games that were two or three decades old even then, while kneeling on top of a stool to reach the controls. Mom thought he had the hots for some girl that worked at the arcade. Maybe she was right? I don't know. Maybe he just really liked the classics.

I rode some of the rides. Old wooden roller coasters that creaked and sounded like death at every turn. Got a t-shirt, and a giant plastic souvenir mug filled with cheap pop. I sort of remember that stuff? I remembered the bearded animatronic pirates. An island of those robots acting out scenes. It was from the days when every park wanted to be Disney World, no matter what the size. They were ancient by the time I saw them. Half mad machines with rusty gears and strange eyes.

I think they were my favorite ride, if that could be considered a ride. Walking a path around an island, walking into mock saloons and watching robots shoot at each other.

Some nights, I dream of that island. I dream of the fireworks they shot at night. I dream of the robots drinking and singing and shooting at each other. I dream of the live bands they would have been playing and the smell of the spilled beer they sold there to the grown-ups. I dream still of the ferry we took from the midway to the island. It cost four tokens.

I feel like someone flicked a match against my
skin.

We pull in and I get this strange feeling, like being in two places at once. Something is under my skin again and I need to cut it out. I can't help but look at everything and feel me now and my younger self, both existing at the same time. Which world do I belong in? Which is more real? The child me who is now a ghost, lost and lonely? Or this teenage me hunting for answers in a broken world?

I feel sick. I feel so sick.

I lean over, dry heaving. I need to vomit this place out of my heart. I need to take all of my memories, everything that's giving me this disconnect, and I need to purge it from my system.

Clara watches me. We are outside of the car and the pines are brushing our heads. Up ahead, the giant shattered neon signs welcome us to the midway. This is a gate that separates our world from the world of the spirits.

I wipe off my face and I see it for what it is. These are the haunted lands. This is where the ghosts go to live, the land of dead memories. The land of past impeding on the present. Everything is alive and full of death at the same time. All of my memories are still walking around behind that sign. My ghosts. The ghosts of my childhood. Wandering.

"You okay?" Clara asks.

"Sure."

"What's up? Can you go on?"

"No. I mean… Take out those fucking flashlights and let's go."

"Come on, don't bullshit me. What's going on with you right now?"

"It's...It's so strange being here now."

"I know. I saw pictures and then that video, but still. Being here? It's so different. It's..."

"Discord," I finish for her. "This world is kind of all broken and smashed up."

"Yeah. Splintered."

"Like broken glass, and I got cut on the sharp edges of the past."

Clara looks at me. "Right." Her gaze is one of concern, and I feel dizzy and off kilter.

"They're sliding under my skin, those glass slivers." Something is waking up inside of me, and my words are poetry. Was this how Casper felt? Before he went missing? Did he dream the same dreams I dreamt; did he have a wild animal in his heart?

Clara sighs, like she doesn't know what to make of me, of what I'm saying. I want her to understand, but I don't think she could ever understand. Never truly, not unless she saw the Dead Snake Tree. Not until she felt poetry rising up inside of her, under her skin, a wild animal that must be cut out to set free.

"Come on, " she says, "Let's go."

She tosses me a flashlight. I turn it on and the light dances around in the night. "When did you snag these?" I say as Clara turns hers on.

"These are my dad's, I snagged them before I snagged you. Crazy fucker, he's always paranoid about shit. Everything in the house practically doubles as a weapon of some sort."

"Yeah."

"You can bash someone pretty good with it. I got a knife, too."

"You think…"

"What?"

"That we're going to… You know?"

Clara thinks. "I don't want to. But yeah. We might need to protect ourselves."

I think back to that video. Whoever it was that dragged those fifteen teens here probably won't be scared of a flashlight. They probably have guns. I really hope we don't get shot.

Clara takes in a deep breath and walks forward a bit, shining the flashlight into the dark beyond the gateway. Shadows scurry out of sight. There are ghosts out there.

Ghosts, or maybe something else, something worse.

Something squirms inside me. trying to tear me apart. Pain crawls across my skin like worms, like someone is sliding sewing needles under my fingernails. Like someone is pulling my muscles too tight.

"Ready?" Clara says.

I'm not ready. I'm not ready. I'm not.

"I guess. Let's go."

We walk forward. Our steps are strong. We don't hesitate even though something inside of me is screaming to get out. Even though every part of me wants to run from here. I see the sign up front, now crooked and collapsing, and we approach the ticket booths lining the front gates and get ready to run inside.

I remember my dad waiting in line with tickets. He got them from the factory for their company picnic they held here every year. That was the only way we could afford to come, when the union paid our way through. I remember him flirting with the ticket lady and mom staring at him like she was going to rip his arm off and beat the ticket lady to death with it. Maybe I should've seen their divorce coming.

These ghosts. They don't go away. They only get stronger with each step. Everything looks the same. Everything looks different. My stomach is burning and screaming. I feel like vomiting again but I ignore it and keep going on. Walking through the gate. We have no tickets. We have no tokens. We walk through anyway. The gate does not stop us. It swallows us every bit and piece of us as we squeeze through, between its teeth.

It doesn't get any easier, the further we go. Each step is haunted. Each breath we breathe is haunted. Am I one of the dead? Am I one of the living? I touch a rusted-out shell of a roller coaster carriage. It is part of the long procession that looks like it was flung from the tracks long ago, lying in the grass like a spine of metal covered in vines.

"Do you remember this one?"

There is a picture of a wolf howling on each of the carriages.

"Yeah. I do."

"Let's keep going. The arcade? Right? It's still a ways."

"I know."

We climb over the carriages. I want to sit in one. I remember my dad and me next to each other. The last thing we ever did together was ride this ride. The last time together. Sit in this seat. Watch the clouds come up to our faces and then plummet down. He laughed. It wasn't often we would see him laugh. Yet, there. There it was, laughter.

"Shit. Hazel? You zoning out on me again?"

"Yeah, no. Sorry."

We move onward. The rest of the park lay spread out in front of us. I want to set fire to all of this. Maybe set fire to myself, and stand on top of the tallest roller coaster. Clara could spread the gasoline before I go up. And then. And then. I would burn it all. Burn myself. My skin would burn like paper burns. The world would burn like all worlds burn.

You can almost hear the kids laughing and running along the midway. You can almost still see them. My childhood. It feels like it wasn't that long ago, and maybe it wasn't? I don't know. I feel some connection to it still. The memory of my dad is there. I want to hate him. I want to forget him. I want to move on. I don't fucking need him.

The Arcade was the place my brother called home whenever we went to the midway. I remember it so well. Casper always pulled us there the moment we walked into the park. It had always been that way. Even though they hadn't changed the line-up of games in over two decades, he didn't care. He wanted quarters. He wanted to play. He was like an addict. We always had to drag him out of there, force him to go on the rides with the rest of us. He would throw tantrums. He would kick and scream until he got his way and we just let him play and play and play.

Eventually, my parents would limit his quarters, make sure he only got a handful, and that he understood this before going in. That way, he was happy; we were happy. He would limit his video game time, and then come out and join us on the rides and have fun together.

Was I happy back then? I don't know. Maybe some part of me was happy. It's hard to remember this, all of this and not feel an empty yearning towards something else. The past? Maybe. My childhood years, before I was a teen? Probably. Something else, something different? I don't know.

I never got this appeal. Video games never really interested me. I guess it was just a difference in our choices of escapism. Some summers I would take a book and sit in the shade and read. I would spend the day reading, just reading. My parents let me, didn't force me to do anything else. I guess they were happy I was reading? Which is weird, now that I think about it.

But my brother. My brother loved this place. Loved placing the quarters in. Loved jumping and gobbling yellow dots and shooting aliens that flew around in weird formations. He loved digging holes in virtual dirt and running from weird pixel monsters. I remember still, younger him, making little replications of these video games using paper and scissors. He would find emulators for them and play them on his computer. He was obsessed.

Oh. My brother. Oh.

I picture him as he is now and I feel a crushing weight on my chest.

I miss him so fucking much.

The Arcade is a low flat building covered in vines. You can see the roof is collapsed. Even from here. Wide open roof letting the light from the moon inside. Clara's walking ahead of me, through tall grass. It goes up to our knees. Spray paint covers the arcade. Geometric shapes with strange letters that curl over each other. Runes made of night. They feel like magic spells that I can't understand.

The light from our flashlights moves over objects ahead of us. More rusted pieces of rides scattered in the weeds.

"You ever notice that we're always going into places like this?" I say.

Clara stops, looks at me. Her flashlight is scattering over the grass.

"Like what?"

"Run down, falling apart. Places without people anymore. All rust and vegetation and shit. Those kind of places?"

A fog rolls in near the ground barely touching the grass. It makes everything look supernatural. Like we've crossed over in to a different world somewhere else. Like in that movie, Spirited Away. Maybe we'll start waiting on old gods from a different world like servants to the dead.

"Yeah, I guess we are, " and Clara shines the flashlight on her face. She looks like the Clara that crawled out of the mirror in that one dream I had years ago, when I was still a freshman. I walked into Clara's bedroom in my dream, and she was gone, and there was a large mirror waiting for me. Clara's reflection was still inside the mirror, waiting for me, smiling a backwards smile. When she pushed against the edges of the mirror, I felt the world shudder and when I woke up, I swore the real Clara was replaced by the mirror Clara for a good month or two. Some days, I still think that's the case. Like today, when her face changes under the light of the flashlight, it makes her into a stranger.

"Weird. But I guess that's just what it's like living here, you know? Everything is run down and broken." She pauses and smiles a little. "I find it strangely beautiful, don't you?"

I nod, and we walk towards the arcade. A muffled sound of crying echoes around us, like what we heard on that email.

I stop. I don't want to go forward. Something bad is going to happen. Something bad always happens. I turn off my flashlight and slink down into the mist, into the grass. Mud clings to my knees, Wet and sticky.

Clara feels strange next to me. I know that dream wasn't real. That there wasn't a mirror Clara and my mind is just freaked out right now. But I can't help it, I can't shake the feeling that it's not really Clara.

"What's up? You okay?"

I lift my head up to the moon. The pines are reaching out towards it. They move. Subtle in the breeze. Waving hands at the sky. The pines are praying to the moon. I can't look at her face, I can't tell her how I'm really feeling. The sound of the crying gets louder. Sobbing. I want to scream, instead I say, "Can't you hear it? Can't you hear the crying?"

I need to cut myself again. I bite my lip and the sharp quick burst of pain abates the feeling inside. The taste of pain washes over me, cleans me. I feel whole now. I hope the feeling will last. Clara kneels down next to me. She looks like Clara again, and I exhale slowly, relieved but still terrified. The sound of crying is still there. Can't she hear it?

"Yeah," Clara says, and swings the flashlight around, shedding light and casting shadows in the dark. No movement, the sound echoes and I feel it in my bones. "Do you think we should call 911 or something? Maybe the cops?"

Everything tenses up again. The pain in my blood rises up once more and I don't know what I want. "Let's take a look first," knowing they won't get here in time if someone is dying and needs help right away. I don't want to be that help, I don't want to see the bodies, but I know that it has to be me. It has to be us. I have no idea why I know that, but I know that. And I hate it so much.

When I stand, I see it. I don't think Clara sees it. She's focused too much on the arcade ahead of us. But I see it. I see it. Two eyes reflecting the moonlight. Two little red ears bobbing. Fox nose. Fox face. Just peeking out from the ends of the grass. Fox face is watching us. The eyes are like white lights, shining directly into my being, carving pieces out of me. Whole pieces being carved out of me with that light.

I wonder if anything will be left of me.

Clara keeps saying we should go but it sounds like she is underwater. She leans down and I stare some more and I want to will her to see the fox. Look at it. That fox. Watch it like I've been watching it. "Don't you see it?" I say, "Don't you see the fox? It's right there. Look at it! It's right there."

Her face obscures everything. "Come on," she says, "Hazel, come on. I don't know what's going on with you? But I need you to stay with me. Come on."

She pulls me up and the fox bounds through the tall grass.

"Don't you see that?"

Clara glances around.

"See what?"

"Never mind."

"No, really. See what?"

I'm numb, but I can move. I know that much.

"Let's go. Come on, let's go."

And we move together. Towards the arcade, under the praying arms of the pine trees.

We walk into one of the many doors in a honeycomb of exits. Scattered through the large open floor are old, dead arcade games. My flashlight dances through the maze of machines.

Vines choke them into silence. Monitors are smashed. Birds made nests in them, disturbed the minute we walk through. They flutter through the collapsed roof up to the moon beyond. I feel their feathers against my skin. It's too dark to tell what kind of birds they are.

Clara walks ahead, slowly investigating with her own flashlight.

Clara looks around. "I don't hear the crying anymore. Did they leave the arcade?"

"I don't know. Should we call the cops now?"

My flashlight moves. Nothing in the light. "Maybe? Though they might want to know why we didn't call them in the first place."

"Yeah. I guess that's right."

We walk further. Something rustles in the shadows, the sound of disturbed leaves and branches like an animal crawling. We shine our lights towards it. Nothing moves in the tall grass.

"You heard that, right?" she asks me.

I nod. Something isn't right here. Something bad is going to happen. I can feel it. I'm afraid one of the machines might turn on and start beeping at us: a ghost begging for quarters to bring it back to life. Each quarter another life, another five minutes to exist before death. I wonder what that says about us. About America.

"Hello?" she calls out.

This is danger. This is dangerous. I want to burn up now. The pain inside of me is a living thing.

"Hello? We're not going to hurt you. We're here to help?"

More rustling. Movement in the grass. The outline of something horrible crawls at the ground. Crawling through the tall grass. Crawling through the weeds. We couldn't see the actual thing itself. Only its outline. Only its movement.

I step back a little and say, "Is that an animal? Like a dog or a bear or something?"

"Whatever it is, it's really fucking big," Clara says and tries to follow it with her flashlight.

"What will we do?"

The light moves with the shadows, trying to capture them with the light. Clara sighs with her entire body, and I feel that in my soul. "Do? I guess we hope it doesn't attack us."

She moves slowly towards the moving outline in the tall weeds. I want to follow, but I'm frozen in my spot. I can't move. I *want* to move. I *can't* move. The past and the present collide now. Had they brought my brother here? Had they brought him to his favorite childhood spot and, done that to him? Did they take him to the arcade to hurt him? Hurt him in such a way that he wasn't my brother anymore? Just a make-believe thing. A fairy tale creature lost in a web of slumber.

"Hazel, come on, please. Come here Hazel."

Clara's standing still. I think she might be close enough that she could see it…actually see it.

But I don't want to come closer. I don't want to see it, whatever it is. I also don't want to abandon my friend.

I suck in my breath. Hold it in. Move forward. I can't leave her alone.

Casper's favorite game was Gauntlet. I remember that. He was always playing it. I remember it screaming at us, every time we walked by. Warning of us of dangers within the mazes. Telling us that "Red Elf Needs Food Badly."

I move towards the outline of something in the grass. Clara is still, stone still, and I see the *Gauntlet* machine planted in the ground. It's in the same spot, and everything is the same and everything has changed. The moonlight dances on the cracked monitor and I still see my brother, ten years old or so with fingers grasped and thumbs pounding, his eyes manic and a smile on his face.

I think that's the last time, last time, I ever, last time, saw, last time, I ever, saw, I saw a smile on his face, I think that was the last time I ever, I saw, a smile, a smile on his face...

And then I'm on the ground. Clara needs my help but I'm on my knees and my head is in my hands and I'm screaming. I don't know what's happening to me. But the scream is coming out. The scream trapped in my blood; the scream pumped through the ventricles of my body… It's out now. It's burning the air. That scream is burning every part of me, and I can't stop. I want to stop screaming, but I can't.

Clara runs over to me, tries to hold me still, tries to keep me calm. She grabs my face with the palm of her hands, and forces our eyes to meet as something electric moves through my body. She leans her head in, tilts her forehead against mine, and whispers in my face. "Clara, Clara, stop it you're scaring me, Clara, please… This is bad enough as it is…"

I'm shaking. My legs, my body. My hands, my fingers.

I'm biting on my tongue. I'm clenching my fists.

"Fuck this place," I say, "Just fuck it."

Eventually I stop and stand up. The grass is still moving in our flashlight beams.

"Fuck it."

And I walk towards it. Clara stands behind and watches. In awe, in fear. She watches.

Butterflies. The first thing I see are butterflies and they scatter the closer I get. At first, I think they're moths, but they're not. The wings are too pretty, like stained glass. Are they monarchs? They almost look like monarchs, but the colors seem slightly off, with the orange close to a blood red and the blacks deeper and darker like an empty pit of night. Their wings are ragged, and their flight patterns feel sinister in a way I can't explain. They fly up from around me, moving over my body.

And it's odd. Even though they are pretty, when you get up and close to them and really see them, they are terrifying. Their heads look like tiny human skulls, with sharp little teeth. Their limbs rustle and click when they move, and they feel like bones dragged across my body. There are hundreds of them, going over my body and flying up to the sky. I'm covered in ants with stained glass for wings.

Eventually they're gone.

I turn and look at Clara and she's walking forward. "The grass stopped moving."

I nod. "Probably just those? Butterflies? But is that right?"

"Yeah. What are they doing here?"

"I don't know."

I was right. I don't want to be right. I shine my flashlight down. I see things in the grass, glimpses in the light. I think I see hair? And maybe a mouth, lips, parted lips? And teeth. I'm pretty sure I see all of that and I don't want to see it. I want to turn around and run away. But I can't. I need to do this. The scream inside may be gone, but the wild animal is still there. The wild animal that wants to be cut out of me.

"Do you see something Hazel? What is it?"

If only it was just the one head.

I want to scream but all those screams before are gone. I want to cut this memory out of my skull. I want to take off this flesh and hang it out to dry somewhere. Like maybe on those trees outside, just hang my limp skin from those trees and then maybe…

Maybe…

Maybe… I'll feel clean and normal and all right again.

Clara's voice, echoing from behind me. Far away, long gone. "We should call the cops."

"Yeah."

"We should call them and go."

"Okay. Right."

I know Clara's right, but my phone is far away and distant. Everything is underwater, it feels impossible to even reach down and grab my Clara, to steady myself against the dizziness that threatens to consume me. Let alone reach into my pocket, grab my phone, and actually start dialing the number for the police. Maybe Clara can do it. Maybe.

Five severed heads. Mixed genders: male, female, whatever. Each of them had the eyes removed and their mouths open. Pried open. Placed open. Butterflies were crammed into every orifice. Their multi-colored wings reflect our flashlights. Five severed heads in a circle. All the faces point directly towards us. Like they knew which direction we were coming from. Like they had been waiting for us to arrive.

I drop to my knees, everything spinning, I have no anchor in the world anymore. "I…I don't want to get any closer. I don't want to be in that circle. I know that sounds stupid, or whatever, but, I just can't. I can't do it."

"That's a good idea, you stay there." Clara's now dialing 9-1-1.

Should we leave? Should we stay here? Is it safe? Is any of this safe? I just want to go back to the hospital. I just want to get back and hug my brother. Maybe curl up against his coma body and sleep with my head on his shoulder like we used to sleep. Back when we had a little bit of cash after we lost the house, and we all shared the same hotel rooms. Back before Dad left for good. I want that. I want us to be in the same place again, arm in arm, waiting for the sun to come up, waiting and waiting without breathing.

Someday the sun will come up again. Someday it will all be daylight again. I just want to wait with him. I know when he wakes up, the sun will never go away again, and we'll never have night again.

She hangs up her phone.

"Okay. We should, I don't know. It's a crime scene. We need to go outside? Maybe? Not touch it? I don't know. Some CSI shit like that. I don't know."

And I walk up and hug her. I know it's not enough to make anything right, but I needed this hug more than anything else in the world. And I had a feeling she needed it, too.

I knew those heads. Clara knew them too. Scattered in ages but all teens, all from our high school. I think they were each one of the missing, one of the unknown. When we step out of the arcade to wait for the police, Clara acts like she hasn't seen anything. Like she expected to see what she saw. It's odd, but I don't know what to say. I'm all broken down and torn apart and put back together again.

"Was there more on that video?" I ask her.

"Oh, what?"

Clara's not looking at me. She's looking at the grass. At the moon. At the praying pines. She's not looking at me and I don't like that. It makes me feel empty somehow. Like I'm a ghost somehow. I want to scream "look at me, look at me! I'm visible I'm real I'm here!"

But then again...

Yeah. I don't know.

Am I real? This doesn't feel real. How could this be real?

"The video, you know. That one that led us here. Was there more to it? More than what you showed me, I mean."

"Oh that. Huh."

She's still looking everywhere else but me. She seems so calm and here I was erupting.

"Yeah, that. Huh. I…I don't know. I can't…I can't think about that. Not right now? Okay?"

I walk up to her. "No, not okay. What do you mean?"

She turns and looks at me and I see her whole face is quivering. I feel like shit, feel like an ass. Why did I say that? Who was I to judge other people's reactions?

"I mean. I don't know anymore. I can't think right now because... fuck. Fuck. Can you think? Fuck. What. What the hell was that? I don't know. Fuck."

Now I turn and I don't want to see her. Or maybe I don't want her to see me? All I know is that I need to be invisible, need to melt into the air. I need to be past tense and just float like memories in a storm. We both sit and wait for the sounds of sirens. Those are the sounds of hope. The sounds of normalcy once again.

I'm in Clara's kitchen with a knife pressed against my arm. My hand is steady. My arm is steady, waiting for the cut. I should've gone back to the campsite. But I can't. I can't do that tonight. Clara asked me to come back and stay another night, and what could I say? After talking to the cops and going over everything, and then going down to the station and talking some more, I needed solidity. I needed something that felt like it was made of real stuff. A life I barely remember, from before dad left and before we were homeless and struggling so damned much. Maybe that life is a lie, or a shadow. I don't know, fuck it. It's what I wanted, you know? That life everyone wants, that everyone sees on television every night or in cartoons or whatever.

Mom and Dad middle class life. Some sort of waking dream we all walk through. But my life doesn't feel like that. My whole life feels wrong. One parent. Not two. No house, no home. Just a tent that gets like a swamp in the rain. And now this. Brother in the hospital, and my childhood wonderland filled with severed heads.

And the butterflies. I think of the butterflies as I press the knife down. Clara's asleep in her skull sleeping bag. It's four in the morning. I feel the edge cut. It hurts. Oh, fucking hell. I lift the blade up and I think of how the butterflies took flight when we got over there, how the butterflies went up into the air. And I feel some release. I feel like my blood is able to scream now and something inside of me lets loose.

I drop the knife with a clank and I fall to the ground with my head in my bloody arm and I'm crying. I hate that I'm crying. I don't want to be crying.

But once the blood started trickling, the dam burst. I'm sobbing like a damned child. Fuck, I grab the edge of the counter. I hold myself steady. I'm a bit dizzy, but not from blood or sleep loss. Just from everything that's happened.

I get about to cleaning it up and then I wonder how I'll ever sleep again.

And if so...what will my dreams be?

When we wake, we get dressed. All of my clothes right now are basically the same clothes. Clara's mom watches me and she has this concerned look on her face. I feel like shit. I want to cut some more but now's not the time. But then again, is it ever the time? I close my eyes. I see the heads. All in a circle, and I don't want to think about it.

Clara's mom walks over to me. "I think we're about the same size. Yeah?"

"I guess so?" I see her standing there, looking me over, sizing me with her eyes, weighing me and judging me like some prized pig. I want to retch. And yes, she is about the same size as me, the same build and everything. Creepy skinny, though I bet hers is from crash diets or whatever, and not from lack of food like my poor ass.

"Clara, what do you think?"

Clara rolls her eyes, her voice dripping with sarcasm that her mom doesn't even remotely pick up. "Sure, Mom. You guys could be twins, or something."

She walks back to her room and I can hear her calling out to me.

"I've got some old things I was going to throw out. You want them?"

I want to say no. I want to run out into the backyard and jump over the fence and run and run and run. Would I ever be able to stop? I want the world to be a blur. I want to run so fast, time stops and it's all amber around me. Frozen and still and holding its breath.

Clara bumps my shoulder with hers.

"Go ahead, I hate to admit it, but she's got good taste."

I know, I can see that. But I don't have good taste and I know I would feel awkward in her suburban mom attire. I would feel like a stranger, like someone pretending to be me. Someone who fails at it. Fails all the time at it. But what else could I say? I needed to get out of these clothes that smelled like fire.

"I guess. Yeah."

My voice is small again. Last night, I needed the sitcom solidity of this house, of this place. I wanted it. But now it feels stifling. It's all so clean. Everything is so nice and neat and nothing is strange or out of place. Even the corny stuff seems chosen so carefully, culled from yard sales for their authentic look. It's all so smothering.

She comes out of the back and the clothes aren't really that bad. Nothing designer that I could see. No mom-jeans or anything like that. She sees my eyes, the look on my face. I guess my face is betraying my emotions.

"Oh, don't worry. These are what I wear when I go out with my friends. We like to hit dive bars and just pretend, well, to not be moms for a little bit. It can be so stifling. Oh dear, don't give me that look. You'll understand when you have kids of your own. Sometimes you need to just get out and be, well, someone else. If only for a small chunk of time."

I take the clothes. And I feel somehow oddly comforted by her admission. That somehow, her life was stifling for her, too. Maybe Clara's mom was someone else once upon a time. She wasn't born into this life. She chose it, and lives it, but needs to shed her skin too. Like something in hiding, wearing the skins of her prey in order to fit in. I understand that.

"Thanks," and I go into the bathroom to get changed.

"Okay. And when you're done, honey, grab a quick snack before we go, okay? I know you gals had a rough time last night with the corpses and everything and the police station. Some food will do you good. And hey, are you sure you want to go to the hospital, and not school? You might get behind on some stuff."

I'm pulling on the pants and I stop for a moment. She's right, but I can't do that. I need to see my brother after last night. He could've been one of those heads, one of the dead. He barely missed out on something horrible. I need to go back and make sure he is still real. I need to make sure he is really there, every part of him. Especially his head.

"I need to go to the hospital."

I button the pants and I hear them whispering in the other room. I wish I could make out what they were saying. I get this unsettling feeling in my stomach. I can't explain it, but something is wrong, and I don't know what that is. Something wrong with Clara, with her mom. More so than the usual icky feeling I got when over at their house. Her mom had always creeped me out, but today it was the worst of it.

"Will you be coming back again tonight? We have something special planned; someone wants to meet you. He wants to meet you both."

I have no idea how to answer that, so I leave the question hanging in the air. I don't know what I want either way. To go back to the campsite? No, I still can't do that. I really can't. Do I want to spend the night next to my brother? I want that. But I don't know. Maybe it might be too much.

I remember the first time I spent the night at Clara's house. We were so much younger. Back then, my parents were still together. Both of them had work. We had a house. Everything felt right. Everything felt normal. I'm sure there were bad times, right? But it feels like they never happened. Like they were completely erased from my memories and only happy ones remained. Even in dreams. In dreams of that time, the worst that happens is dinner is burnt and we order pizza. That's it.

I remember even then Clara's house felt strange. Off somehow. Like it was too perfect. It felt like walking into the twilight zone every time I stepped inside. I didn't like that feeling. But I liked Clara. I liked her a lot.

Her parents were...okay. And her mom, well, she has always got under my skin. It got worse after my dad left. After we were homeless. Her mom became even creepier and creepier. Like she wanted to adopt me. To take me in. Make me her little cuckoo child and nurse me in the dark.

Anyway... That first time was the strangest. I remember waking up and not knowing where I was. I walked through the house. Clara and I were asleep in the living room, just the two of us. I was so confused, and I wanted to find my mom and dad, I wanted to find out where I was. I went into each room, lost, wandering through the maze.

I remember walking up the stairs and looking into each room for them. And I'm not sure if I remember this right or not. It feels strange. Clara's parents were gone. And when I got back downstairs, Clara was gone. The sleeping bag was still on the floor, but it was empty. I was scared and alone.

I heard a sound, like a record playing old scratchy music sung in a different language. Strange and lost and haunted. My thoughts were drowned out by that sound. Everything spun around me. Soon, the sound stopped and I stopped. I just sat with my knees to my chest wondering if my world had broken and I was drifting through it like a boat on a storm-filled ocean. Like a painting hung in my parent's room at the time.

Eventually I remembered where I was. The rest is all fuzzy. They must've come back? At some point? Or maybe they'd never left? Or maybe it was just a dream I had? Or maybe I walked home and I don't want to remember because it was a moment of shadows and lightning and I don't like those moments.

Nobody likes moments like those.

They drop me off in front of the hospital. Dylan stands outside, hands in pockets, spine against the brick wall. Running around him and screaming where the little girls with bird masks on their faces.

I see him and it makes me want to run, it makes me want to stop everything and leave. Fuck him. I don't need this. I don't need him. Fuck him.

I want to get back into the car. I want to tell them not to go, that I've changed my mind. But when I turn around, the car's gone. I stand there, back to him. Back to the girls. Looking for the car. I can't even see it in the distance. I hear the laughter of the bird girls playing. And I think of Dylan killing that little bird. And my fingers clench into a writhing fist. I want to hit him or push him away before he touches one of those little girls. He can't hurt them. He better not fucking hurt them. I will not let him.

I turn around, seething and ready to knock his head off if it comes down to it. I am done with this, with him, with everything.

He flicks a cigarette and almost hits one of the little girls. Just barely misses.

I want to hit him and punch him and fucking stab him and make him go the fuck away. I've had enough. I've seen enough. I don't need anything else; I just need him to stop and go away already. Fuck! Just stop and go away.

"I won't be here long, so you can stop freaking out already," he says. He smells like gasoline and fire. He looks terrified when he speaks, his eyes are wide, and his teeth chatter a little when he talks. He looks up to the clouds. As if looking for real birds. Like they were watching, following him. Spies in the skies.

"What is it?"

He nervously wrings his hands, and his eyes keep darting about, looking. Looking. His nervousness feels dangerous, like he could explode at any moment. "Nothing. I mean something. I mean…shit."

"What? What the fuck?"

"The campsite."

"What about it? Dylan. Come on."

"It burned. All of it. It burned."

I push him and he almost falls on one of the girls. They laugh and scream and act like it was nothing but a game.

"What the? I didn't do anything, I…I tried to stop it. The woods almost burned down. I was asleep, all right? Fucking hell, and they were… They were dousing me. Don't you get it? They were pouring gasoline on me. I was supposed to die."

I feel nothing inside. Part of me wishes that he would have died after everything that happened between the two of us.

"Yeah? You call the cops?"

He stands up.

"They came and all that, but I don't remember calling. I don't remember much. I only remember running from the fire because I didn't want to die. I'm so sorry. If I could have saved some shit or stopped it, I would have, but I didn't want to die. Okay? Okay?"

A bird-masked little girl walks up to him and says, "Here," and hands him a lily.

He takes it.

"Now, say thank you to me."

He thanks her.

I use this moment to walk past them, walk into the double glass doors, and walk into the maze of hospital halls beyond. I'm full of night; this heavy presence is sitting on my chest again. I need air. I need to scream again. I need to cut again.

I need I need I need I need I need

Mom's sitting up next to my brother. She's dressed him in pajamas from home. I feel odd looking at him. It's like he's going to sit up and start sleep-walking around. The oxygen mask on his face makes everything seems even stranger. She's reading some magazine and picking at a salad.

"You hear about what happened?"

She picks some more and laughs a little. "Yeah, the campsite, right. The cops called me earlier. I guess my photos were scattered about half-burned. All of those memories, now all charred and ash. Fuck."

I don't know what to say to this, to anything. I just stand next to her and put my arm over her shoulders. She puts her head against my chest.

I feel so odd lately. I don't know who I am anymore. Is this woman even my mom still? Everything is so wrong and upside down. "Dylan told me about it."

"Yeah. He was supposed to watch it."

"I know. He smelled like gasoline."

I see my mom's hands change. She pushes my body away, slowly. Her face is bright red. "Fuck!" she screams and slams the salad on the floor. Pieces of it scatter. The plate smashed. "Fuck! Why? What did...I just don't. I don't get it."

I still don't feel like I trust him. He could've just been bullshitting me to get away with starting the fire. No way I could trust him ever again. "He said….. Someone was dousing him. Trying to kill him."

Mom shakes her head and then stands up. She violently shoves the chair against the wall and kicks it a few times, screaming and yelling. My brother doesn't budge, doesn't wake up. His machines still make the same beep beep sound and nothing changes. Nothing happens.

I want her screaming to wake him up. Maybe that would give us a catharsis we need so badly. We need something so badly. Our whole family has been drowning for so long, barely rising our mouth up to gulp air before we are dragged back under again. Now there is someone standing on a boat, pushing our heads down.

"Fuck!" she screams again. "No, it was Dylan. I'm so fucking stupid. I should've listened to you, right? I mean. There were danger signs and everything and I thought he was such a nice boy, and you guys broke up because of stupid high school shit, right? I mean. It wasn't that. It wasn't that, was it? I wanted to keep you away from all of that. I mean it's everywhere, but here I am, pushing you into that fucking lion's jaw. I'm just… Fuck I'm so glad you didn't get eaten. What if he had burned you up, too?"

I don't say anything. I just hug my mom. She starts crying and I hold her still. She sobs against me, apologizing over and over again. Eventually she stops and wipes her face and pats my chest like this was all something temporary, something that would go away after a while.

We don't say anything. Instead, we both bend over and start cleaning the plate pieces and salad scraps off the floor. The black and white tiles are smooth against our hands. We're silent, but it's okay. Saying something now would make everything real. I didn't want it to be real. Down here, picking up the pieces and cleaning the floor felt so normal and mundane. That maybe if we held our breaths and didn't speak, I could will this to be our reality. We're in a home again; we're a family again, and we're just cleaning up a mess in our kitchen. Maybe my brother is upstairs acting like the surly fucking asshole that he is listening to music and that is it. That is all we need. That is all this moment could be.

Eventually, it ends. Eventually it's all clean and we stand up and there is his body in pajamas, hooked up to machines. Eventually, we see the hospital room and everything else inside of it and our world comes back fuzzy and dead and reminds us of who we really were. Of the life we really lived.

That was the problem with reality, isn't it? It's always there. Even if you want it to go away and leave you the fuck alone, it has this problem of sticking around. Of never listening to you, even when you ask it to go away oh so nicely.

I change my mind and tell Clara's mom I'm sleeping at the hospital tonight. She acts concerned, acts like my mom or something. But I'm not an orphan. I have a mom I love and a brother I love and they need me here. She doesn't quite get it; she tells me she's worried about my mental health. I try and be polite, but it's hard being polite. I want to throw the phone against the wall and scream and scream and scream. I know if I go back to that house tonight, I'll be cutting myself in the kitchen again. I can't do that.

Clara calls a little later and wants to know if we're still going out.

"No," I say, "I'm sorry..."

"I know. It's okay."

But her voice? It doesn't sound okay.

"I need to be here. After seeing that..."

"No, it's okay. I'll solve this all on my own, and I'll save those people and everything and it will be all me. You understand? I can't stand by and let this shit happen. I can't. Fuck."

"You okay?"

A pause. I can hear her breathing and it sounds like she's drowning. Maybe we're all drowning.

"No. I mean... No. I saw it."

"What?"

"That motherfucking tree. I saw it in my dream."

I look over at my brother. I see his chest rising up and down, up and down, up and down. His little plastic mask is fogging up and his eyes dance under the lids in REM sleep. The pajamas look so strange on him, so loose on his emaciated body. I feel so strange looking at him. Did he have that dream? Did he dream of the dead snake tree?

"It's okay," she says, "And you don't have to worry about this anymore, I've got this under control, and can do it all by myself. You understand? I'm going to stop it all from happening, and I don't need your help. You don't even care, anyway, so I'm on my own."

"Okay." I am just done with Clara, done with all of this. I just want the horrors to be over already, for my brother to be awake and okay already.

And I close my phone and then turn it off. I can't do this anymore tonight.

It's my turn to watch and read while Mom sleeps. I don't even know what we're looking for anymore. What sign would be a good sign? What would be a bad sign? I put the book down for a second, reach my hand over and place it on his chest. I can feel it: his heart beating. It's so warm—his skin and everything else.

I wonder what worlds he's dreaming of, if he's creating new universes in his sleep. If he wakes up, would that entire world just die out? Would it blink out of existence? Or maybe his dream is a viral dream, and maybe we're all dreaming about his dead snake tree dream, and it spreads out, and this won't stop until he wakes up?

I don't know. I know I don't want to go to sleep. I'm going to try and stay awake. I don't want to dream anything. I'm afraid of that tree, I'm afraid I'll dream of those heads. I don't even know what I'm really afraid of. Everything seems to have fear inside of it, lying in wait. Everything I touch gives me tingles and goosebumps and I'm not sure why.

I just want to be someone else...be *somewhere* else...be *anything* else...

This reminds me so much of the Safe House from when I was just a little cutting girl surrounded by all these other girls with problems. The same hospital walls, the same orderlies, the feeling of hopelessness, of people trying to help you heal but only making everything worse. Thinking about it now is a bitter fruit on my tongue. Yes, we were broken and damaged and our parents were terrified of us hurting ourselves and everyone around us.

But we were so young, just little girls. Not even teenagers yet. We didn't deserve to be in that place, haunting those halls, trying to get well. Just like my poor brother didn't deserve to be here, at this place, struggling to stay alive.

We were trapped and escape was some distant far away dream. Even if you got over the walls and past all the orderlies, you had the forest to contend with, and the fact you were miles and miles away from civilization.

Somehow, this is the same way. Trapped with damaged girls. No escape. Clara's mom even reminded me of one of the therapists who liked to control all of us. She saw herself as a mentor, as a leader. As someone who owned our minds and played with them. Stacey jokingly called her Nurse Ratchet. Which I didn't get at the time, but later, I saw *One Flew Over the Cuckoo's Nest* and I understood.

I guess that's what it's always like in places like these. Places where well-meaning people sent you to get healed. A maze of confusion, of feeling lost, of never being well again, never being yourself again. It's so painful to think about now, yet so powerful. We had each other, that was key. And now? My brother has me and my mom. And in a way, we can survive this, if we survive it together.

I can't help it. I sleep. It's almost dawn and sun creeps up across the ceiling. Mom's still asleep. I was supposed to wake her up hours ago and trade shifts. But I couldn't. I wanted to stay awake. I wanted to fight through the gauntlet of exhaustion. Come out the other side of it all ready to go through the day. But...I drift. My eyes close without me being able to do one damned thing about it. The world shifts around me. I see a baby fox sitting on my brother's chest and I can't help but think 'what's going on...?'

And then I'm dreaming.

12

I don't dream of the Dead Snake Tree. I don't dream of much of anything. I dream of water. It's not like I was swimming or drowning or anything like that. But rather, I am water. Or maybe the dream itself is water? Water. I remember water everywhere. Moving, flowing. Nothing else but dark water. It is empty water. No fish; nothing at all.

When I wake up, I try and remember anything else other than water, but it slips away from me like a wave on a lonely beach, where the sun had already set and left a bruised sky behind.

I look over and Mom's awake. I feel bad about not waking her up and I want to say sorry or something. It seems like she doesn't care really anyway. She smiles a loose crooked smile and hands me a tray of breakfast and tells me to eat up. And I do.

As I eat, I look at her and look at my brother. I don't know how much longer I can stay here. But where else can I go? I am both trapped yet not trapped. I want to leave, but guilt will follow me with every step. My family needs me. We all need each other. Especially after we lost all of the photos and our few possessions we had left in that fucking fire. That *fucking* fire. Why couldn't it have been me? Why couldn't I have been doused with gasoline and set on fire?

Inside me something stirs. My heart crackles. Embers. Brief flames licking my bones. I picture the pine trees swaying in the breeze as fire lights their branches, the pine cones popping.

I think about that and I think about how it would feel to have my skin burn up like that, and have little charred pieces and ash flutter away from my bones. I think about the burning. I think about the cutting. Maybe if I poured lighter fluid in my cuts and set them on fire, I wouldn't feel so empty and broken on the inside. Maybe then I would be purged of all that screaming inside of me. The flame would take care of it. It would burn it all out of me and then... And then...

I have no idea who I would be anymore. I guess that's okay. Isn't it? Yes, I think so. It's okay. The fire is me and I am the fire and that's all that I need to know. The one truth of the universe. We all catch fire.

After I have some coffee and she sees I'm done with my eggs, my mom clears her throat like she's going to talk. She looks down at her hands, spread out on the empty tray in front of her. "They're moving your brother tonight."

I can't believe it. I can't hear what my mom is saying. It sounds absurd. She can't be serious; she must've heard them wrong. "Moving? Where are they moving him? He can't go...I mean...right? They can't, right? They can't take him away from us, from our family."

She's touching her fingers to her knuckles, a nervous tick she's relied on all these years. She did that when she told us we lost the house. She did that when she told us Dad was leaving us for another family in the hills. She did that when he was presumed dead or something by some asshole cop or detective or whatever.

"What's going on? Mom?"

"I don't know. I don't know. They didn't tell me or anything. They're just going to do it and we don't get a say in the matter."

I lean over and place a hand on hers to get her fingers to stop moving. "Do we have to move and sleep elsewhere?"

"We can't follow him. Where they're taking him, we can't follow him."

"Why not?"

"I don't know. Something about our lack of insurance. I don't know."

I look over at him and I see his oxygen mask is gone now. When did that happen? His lips are black. His skin is blue. His eyes are no longer moving. His chest is no longer moving. When did that happen?

"Is…" I put a hand over my mouth. I don't want the words to come out. I want to push them back inside me, forever floating in my lungs. "Is he? Is he dead?"

Mom laughs and it's such an odd sound. Her face looks wrong. I don't like her face right now. I think of the water in my dreams. I think of the fire from before. And I think about how we've been drowning so much, how we've been under all this water for so long. Is the water on fire? When we lift our heads up and climb onto the boat, will we be on fire? Is that's what is on the other side of the water? Fire?

"No," she says and for a moment her face was a normal mom-face. It's a face I haven't seen since my brother left. "No, he's alive, and they want to make sure he stays alive. So, they're going to take him to the Sleep Room."

"Sleep Room?"

She nods. "I guess it's only for him right now? But it's filled with nothing but beds and this staff…this staff who will keep him alive. I wish they would've asked? But if they can keep him alive…"

I pull my hand back and run it through my hair. "Okay then. And we can't see him?"

"I don't know," and the she hides her face in her hands. "They said no, oh god, oh fuck. I'm so sorry, Hazel, it's all my fault. It just makes me so angry to feel so fucking useless! So angry and this is so unfair. All because I attacked a fucking nurse. The stupid kid had no idea on how to find a vein and they kept sticking him over and over again. He should've done it right the first time!"

Her hands move down. Her face is fierce. This face is frightening.

"Fuck. I'm his goddamned mom. I have rights! I have to see my little boy. I lost him… Oh, I just lost him and just got him back. Hazel… Hazel? They can't take him away from us again. They can't! Fuck this place and its damned greed."

I look over at my brother. How is he even still alive now? I have no idea. "Where are you going to go? I mean, where are we? We have nowhere to go."

She nods. "I know. I think that's it. I think they're sick of housing these smelly drifter types. Fuck."

"Wait." I pull out my phone. My mom starts to speak and I hold up a finger.

"Clara? Yeah. Can my mom spend the night tonight too?"

And that was that.

Five or six nurses come in and they're all dressed in black funeral scrubs. They wear strange masks over their faces. Their hands are covered in silver gloves. The pick him out of the bed heave-ho and place him on a gurney they had waiting next to the bed. Even though their movements are violent, my brother does not stir, not even a little bit. They tie him in with leather straps and his mouth is still black but his eyes are now wide open. For a moment I think he's awake, but then I see they're not moving. They're just staring straight ahead, not looking at anything.

I want to scream. This isn't right. None of this feels right at all. And I get this sinking feeling that this will be the last time I see him and I try so damned hard not to cry.

I turn my head and they wheel him away. I feel Mom's hand on me pulling me into a hug. We don't move. Not for a moment. Not forever. We stand and we're frozen and it's okay in a way. We're still here, right? Still here. Even though he's not. Shit. Fuck.

My head out of the water, gasping for air. The whole ocean is on fire. Something is pulling my legs down and back underwater I go. I'm drowning? Yes. I look over and my mom's being pulled down too. We're sinking down, down, down into the clear empty water. If I look up, I can see the flames, orange and red, filtering into the water. I look over at my mom, look down at my feet, but I can't see what's pulling us under or where we're going. Now I can't breathe, so, I fight to get up, to get my way up, but they pull more. The fire waits for us and all I want to do is breathe and rest for a moment and breathe...

Me and Mom are on the roof of the hospital. The sun is clear overhead and the sky's filled with tiny stratus clouds. We can see every part of the city. The pines, and the midway, and the large lake that looks like a giant mirror. And we can see the roads filled with tiny cars that look like toys. And then the mall, and the shops, and then the different districts and the schools. The birds sit and rest on telephone wires looking at us. The birds watch us watch them.

My mom stands up. "I am so tired, I just can't do this anymore," she says with arms outstretched to the sun.

"I am too. So tired and worn out. Did they even tell you where this Sleep Room is?."

"No. They're secretive."

"Yeah, really secretive. Stupid if you ask me. Why can't we see him? We're family. Ethics my ass."

"This sucks."

"Yeah."

Mom sits back down, joining me on the ledge. We both look like we're going to jump. If only it were that easy. What would jumping do? It wouldn't do anything. We would probably float down like feathers and nothing would have changed at all.

"Clara."

"Yeah?"

"What's her house like?"

I think about it for a moment.

"Like something out of a sitcom."

Mom laughs at this.

"Oh, so we're going to be living in *Growing Pains* or some shit like that?"

"Yeah," I say, and then we look at each other.

"What crazy, crazy stuff. I don't know if I miss that life at all.

That happy, upper-middle-class dream. It just seems so...fake. Like everyone is trying to be someone else, someone made of plastic and Styrofoam."

"You sound like a member of QAnon," I smile to let my mom know I was teasing, "Like any moment now and you will say that middle class dream was invented by lizard vampire Freemasons or something." And then I pause for a moment. I feel like I need to be honest for some reason. "I miss the stability."

"Yeah, that was nice, all things considered."

We look back out over the city. Those birds, still on the wires, are still looking directly at us. This unsettled feeling hits me as I remember Dylan crushing one with his hands. Maybe Dylan was right?

No. Dylan's not right... Thinking like him is dangerous. His way lies in conspiracy theories and madness.

Mom points at the cut I made on my arm. Her look is one of both concern and alarm, and I hate that this hurts her. What I do, what I have to do. I don't want to hurt her, but I need that release. "What happened?"

I don't want to lie but she's been through enough lately. She doesn't need to know I'm cutting again. That would crush her. I can tell, eyes panicked now, on the verge of tears.

I close my eyes as I say this, unable to look at her, to lie right to her face. "Oh. Right when we went to that, um, place. You know… When we found the heads? I must've got caught on a wire or something."

"Yeah. That. I'm not happy about that. I can't lose you too." Her voice wavers and I open my eyes and she's on the verge of tears.

I lean my head down so my hair is over my face. "I know." I don't want to be seen. I feel small. Tiny. "I won't do that again. Okay?"

Mom rubs her knuckles on my scalp.

"I know, sweetie, I know. God, it's been so long since I've seen Clara's mom, way too long since we've hung out. She must think I'm such a mess, right? Single mom, homeless all that. She's going to be so fucking judgmental, I can tell, she was always like that before. Gossiping about everyone behind their backs, I can't believe I used to play along with that. Shit."

I don't think I've seen her like this ever. Something is breaking inside of her.

"Sorry. Damnit. I just...I don't know. So, do you think she'll like me? As a person now? Fuck. Now that I've changed so much? Fuck. I bet she's exactly the same, and hasn't changed a bit, hasn't she?"

"She's just a mom and stuff. I'm sure it'll all be cool."

I reach over and place my hand on my mom's back. She's close to crying, and I know I have to calm her down, let her know it's all going to be okay. She doesn't have to know Clara's mom creeps me the fuck out. Hell, they might even still get along. Mom could use a friend now.

"Fuck. I don't care. Fucking hell."

The birds scatter and fly off. I stand up and walk towards the stairs leading down off the roof. As I cross the big helipad, I see a helicopter in the distance coming towards us. I motion to my mom to follow me, to go back inside and away from this endless sky.

The blades whir over our heads and as we descend into the hospital just in time. There is yelling as we close the doors, as we climb down over the metal steps quickly, quickly. We don't want to wait and see what's happening, see who's being brought in… It couldn't be good. They were shouting... Not good at all. Shouting in hospitals is always a bad sign.

I was so young when I first started cutting myself. I remember what brought it on. It was all this tension in the air around us. And my parents... All that fighting. We still had a house at that time, and I kept dreaming that the house was on fire. When I woke up, I would forget where I was, completely disoriented, and in a panic, I would run around trying to save everything, thinking that the house was actually burning up. After a few moments of packing, I would realize it was just a dream, and this feeling was the dream hanging around like a ghost in my skull.

That was when I started doing it. I was cutting to get the dreams out of my head. To keep my house from catching fire.

It was a ritual. It was a rite of dreams becoming more than reality. Of existing outside of myself and being outside of my body. I would cut down. I would feel the pain, the release and I'd feel like something was changing. Maybe it changed inside of me. Maybe it changed outside of me.

But I knew, I knew my ritual would keep us safe, would keep the house from catching fire. Every dream. Every time. Walking down the stairs. One step at a time, I could feel that wood against my toes and remember the cloudy way my head felt. Still swimming with dream. Reaching for the knife, usually a steak knife, and cutting. Again, and again, and again. My ritual. My way of keeping everything safe.

And then Mom hearing the noise. Maybe it was like the fifth time? Maybe later than that? But she came down those stairs and saw me. Watched what I was doing. Ran over, and grabbed the knife. Then she helped me clean. She was in shock. She was covered in tears. I hated myself then, I saw myself in her eyes, and I hated myself. I remember whispering "help" over and over again and Mom looking at me and hugging me.

"We'll get you help," she said. "We'll help you stop this."

She took me to bed all bandaged up. And Dad screamed. And they yelled. And she blamed all their fights and problems for me cutting myself. That I was acting out because I felt lost. Because he didn't care enough for me or she didn't or something. I didn't tell her about the dreams. I didn't tell her about the burning house.

I couldn't.

How could I?

How could she understand?

Their reality was made of metal and fire. Mine was made out of symbolic things. Symbols constructed out of shadows and pieces of night.

The help Mom promised was only kind of helpful. It was this place deep in the woods in a big old house: The Safe House. Hiding from the rest of the world, a bunch of pre-teen girls with problems sitting around a table and talking at each other. We threw our words out and listened in awe at the tragedies we'd constructed for ourselves. One girl cut, another starved herself, and another was a firebug. Maybe we were all the same. Or maybe we were all different. We traded stories like old collectors. We commented, refined. Made the drama bigger and more interesting. We all wanted to be interesting. We were all afraid of being invisible to each other.

We needed each other somehow. It helped a little, I guess? I didn't cut for a few years after getting back. Then I did it again for a little while, always in secret. Always in places where they would never see and never find. I didn't want to go back there. The one girl almost killed her sister with the fire she set. The others? All different. Some sticks and bones and I was frightened of the skeletons.

The need to cut slowly went away. Even though more problems piled up around us, that desire ebbed and disappeared. And eventually, it began to feel like it was something that happened to someone else. Like I stole memories from some other girl's sleeping head and I claimed them as mine.

And then...my brother went missing. My brother came back. The urge returned, but the dreams did not. I couldn't claim I was cutting to prevent a future. I was cutting to remove myself. To become someone else. I was cutting because this skin is the wrong skin and this blood is bad blood. I was trying to get outside of this body and find some other shell.

This time, I was cutting to burn the house down.

It was the only way to be free.

My one and only friend from my stay in that house deep in the pines was Stacey. She was there for trying to drink Drano and bleach and sometimes she would eat clay. She said it all tasted like colors, that she was trying to get all the reds and oranges inside her body. It was the only way to complete the rainbow she had clinging to her skeleton. Some people thought she was the craziest. I thought she was the sanest. That should tell you something about me right there.

I'm broken.

I'm so broken.

You can't fix me. I know that. I know that the only way to make things better is to set it all up in flames and start over again when the ashes settle. And I know that the only person who understood this was Stacey. At the time, I didn't know what I wanted. I thought I was preventing destruction. That I was making the world less chaotic with each cut being like a prayer.

But Stacey? She looked at me and said it so plain and simple.

"You want to be reborn. You want to be a new girl."

And she was right. At the time though? I didn't think she was right but I liked her company. She was my Clara when I was locked up in the pines. And I was her friend.

When they finally dismissed me and said it was time to go home, pronounced me cured and no longer a danger to myself and others, she held me close and we promised to write to each other. Pinprick on thumbs, blood pushed to blood. A promise sworn. Such empty words. Such broken air. We never did.

The minute I got outside? The minute I was out of those doors? The last thing I wanted to do was write to anyone from that point in my life. I didn't want to be reminded of any of that. I was free again. I thought I didn't want to cut anymore. I thought maybe I was normal again.

And then?

My dad left.

Everything spun away and broke apart and it was like living on shattered glass.

I want to run through the sunlight in the Safe House. I want to run with arms outspread. I want to run with Stacey behind me giggling. I want Allison to chase us with her wheelchair, laughing all the while. The place was horrible. The place was wonderful. All those girls broken in ways that I felt some kind of strange sisterhood with, Stacey even more than any of the others. We traded our personal horror stories back and forth and felt an awe with each other. The cutting. The devouring.

I want to be back there. Even though they forced me to eat. Even though they tied me down for a while to keep me from cutting my skin off, peeling it a little at a time. There was something there in that large mansion. The way the wood sang us to sleep at night, like tiny drums.

We were dangerous to ourselves, but never to others. That self-annihilation was something I yearned for, and no one understood outside of the Safe House. Here, I felt lonesome and in the darkness. But not there. Not in the Safe House. With others, I ran in the light. We ran towards our own personal fires. We shed our ghosts like skin. We became the light ourselves. And it was beautiful. So beautiful. And Allison led the way.

Her ghost is with me even now, all those years later. I can feel her, just out of the corner of my sight, waiting in the shadows and watching over me. She keeps me sane, keeps the loneliness away.

Yes, Allison is dead now. But I don't feel like I can talk about that just yet.

We're on our way to Clara's house. The world is going by like Morse code. House, house, tree, house, house, telephone pole. I think, this is it. This car is the only place we can call home right now.

I want to break the windows and yell. I want to kick shit and scream. My mom drives and I can tell she's one step away from screaming too. I wonder how much one family can take.

My thoughts drift to the other night and the heads. I can't. Not right now.

Instead, I pull out my phone and I flip through Facebook feeds looking for Stacey. I need to talk to someone else about all this. Someone who would understand. Clara? Clara couldn't understand. She was too well-adjusted to understand this sort of thing.

That, and I want Stacey to be okay. I want to find her and know that she survived it, all of it, and she was alive and thriving and healthy and well. The last thing she told me was that she was going to drink gasoline and light herself up from the inside out. She was going to vomit her whole insides out just to see where the rainbows grow. She told me last time her mother was a wolf and she wanted to stab her a few times just to get the wolf to come out of her. To see that it was real.

I need her to be sane now, to be normal now. I need her to be fine now. More than anything else, more than even seeing Clara and all that. I need her to be one who survives, not one who succumbs.

"We're almost there. You should probably put that away."

I nod. I can't find her. Why can't I find her? I don't want her to be dead. Please don't be dead.

I put my phone in my pocket and hold my breath.

We pull up. Clara and her mom are waiting for us on the porch, smiling and waving. I feel this odd sinking inside of me like I have a shipwreck in my stomach. I slink down in my car seat so they don't see the look on my face.

"Woah, she looks like a Stepford wife. And to think: I was able to get out of all that shit with my sanity intact."

"Yeah," I say and look away from her, away from Clara and her mom, and just stare down the street. Beyond the edges of the streetlamps and the headlights is an inky darkness. I wonder if Stacey is out there, in the darkness, alone and terrified. And I want to find her and save her. I want to save everyone, and maybe if I do, yes, I can somehow save a piece of myself.

I'm not even in the door when Clara's shoving a tablet in my face.

"Was it you?" she demands.

I see the picture and it hits me like shrapnel.

The heads. Each one in a circle, the picture taken far enough back that you can see the circle. But it's close enough that the tall grass doesn't obscure the faces, or the butterflies with wings sticking out of mouth and eye holes. Everything is spinning and I can't make it stop. When was this picture taken? I want to cut this new feeling out of my stomach. I need to do it. Dig a knife in, dig out whatever is making me feel this sick…

"No," I almost whisper, barely defiant, "No. Look at it."

"I don't...I don't want to look at that anymore."

"Then get it out of my face, please. I don't want to look at it either."

She turns the tablet off and puts it on the table.

"The picture was daylight," I say, "I was in the hospital today."

"All day?"

"Fuck, Clara. Yes, all day! I don't need this shit right now. Please, don't. Not right now."

Clara looks angry. Like she has her own rages inside. Maybe I should cut them out of her too? Then we would make a great pair. Two teenage girls with stomachs ripped out and blood all over. Intestines unwrapped like presents. Looking for something living inside, something trying to claw its way out.

"You don't need my shit, but you need my house? Is that it? You want to come here and play pretend? Pretend like you have all of this?"

My mom is out in the garden walking around with Clara's mom. I want to run out there and tell her we need to go. That we have to get out of here. But where would we go? We couldn't go back there...to anywhere. We had no there or where or any of that to go back to.

"No, it's not. Why are you acting like this? This isn't like you."

She turns away from me, paces around the room. Her body moves like an animal. Like it's hungry. Like it's prowling. Like a caged tiger glancing over at the glass and licking its lips. And I know what it's thinking. It's thinking I look tasty. I look good enough to eat.

"Come on. What is this?" I try again.

She stops.

"Dylan came by today."

Fuck. Fucking hell. Fuck it.

Clara's looking at her hands.

I think I'm supposed to speak now? But what can I say? Dylan came by and did something? Did he try to set Clara on fire too? What was going on here? And the pictures. Strange how it all fits together. I was the only one not around. How could it fall back on me?

"Aren't you going to say something?" Clara's eyes accuse me.

I try to contain my seething anger, rising up inside of me. I want to fucking cut; it's like an itch under my skin. "Like what? What did he even do? Or want, or what?"

She shakes her head. "Nothing. I guess."

I practically scream in her face. "Nothing?"

"Fuck." Clara rolls her eyes, frustrated with me. "Yes, nothing. Nothing Nothing nothing." She's biting on her nails now, not glancing at me. I feel the lie between us, and it pisses me off even more than I ever thought possible. That itching under my skin is stronger now, I need to slice I need to cut I need...

Staying here was a bad idea. We should be in the hospital watching over my brother. Sleep, sleep, sleep… Someone needs to protect him while he sleeps. I need to protect him.

"You're lying. If it was nothing, you wouldn't be like this."

"You saw him today, yeah?"

"At the hospital. He came by to tell us that someone set the camp on fire. You happy? They burnt us out and forced us to be out on our own and Dylan couldn't fucking stop it, he's useless. And then? They moved my brother. The doctors took him away from us and we can't see him."

Clara's eyes soften. Just a moment. Like a crack of light in the shadows.

"What? They moved him? Can they do that? Is that legal?"

"I guess it is."

"I'm sorry," she says this in a way that sounds uncertain, like she doesn't know what feelings are, and she's not sure which ones are which. If she could construct them and display them when needed. "Look. He came by here looking for you and he really pissed my mom off."

"He did? What happened?"

"He… I dunno. He threatened us. He kept yelling at my mom, telling her that he had to see the Poet, that he needed to see the Poet. It was so terrifying, he smelled like woodsmoke and gasoline."

"I know."

"We thought... he was trying to burn us down. Mom called the cops and they had to drag him out of here."

"Clara, I'm so sorry..."

She stands up and places her hand out, her palm up. I put my hand in her hand and she helps me stand up.

"Shit," she says, "The guys you date... What the hell's up with that?"

I laugh.

"I don't know. I really pick winners."

"Yeah, you do. Come on, let's have dinner and then figure all of this out later."

"Got it. Slumber party?"

"I don't know about you but I'm not up to playing *Scooby-Doo* tonight. Not after what we found."

I hug her for a second. I needed that. Something warm and human and not dead inside. I hug my mom like I'm taking care of her. But right now, I needed to be taken care of. I needed to be the one who was helpless. If even only for a second. So, I let Clara hold me like she's lifting me up to the sky, keeping me safe from everything in the world. I need that. I need to be safe.

Eventually we part and it's okay. Sometimes even a little bit helps out.

"Have you heard your son's poetry?"

Clara's mom is talking as she dishes us up. Nothing extravagant, but still, it's warm and it's good. And hey, it wasn't cooked on a grill or over a campfire, or pulled out of a vending machine or a dumpster by McDonald's or Pizza Hut.

My mom looks shy and broken and out of place. She's a different person here, a person I barely recognize. She utters a fake laugh at fake jokes. She sparkles a fake sparkle, and tilts her hands in ways that exaggerate form and detail.

I wonder if she's putting on a show? Or is she becoming herself? And yet, at this comment, the mention of Casper's poetry, that cocktail party mask slips a little bit. Nervous, my real mom shining through. It's heartbreaking.

"What are you even talking about? He's in a coma, he's, he's. What poetry?"

"Oh, he wrote some really interesting poems, I find them kind of surreal. You know what I mean? The Poet really liked them, you know. He thought he was the most gifted, almost as gifted as his daughter."

Mom looks bewildered and crushed, and for a moment she seems to be trying that cocktail party mask on again, slipping back into that fake happy cheerful attitude.

I know it's going to break her, that this whole evening could break her, so I butt-in and take over the conversation. "I knew he wrote some. Well, kinda. I just found out. How did you know?"

Her mom stops serving for a moment. She looks sort of sad and wistful. "Oh, right. I just, I heard it. At poetry readings? I always wonder why you guys never showed up. Did he not tell you about them?"

"No," I say, "He never told us." That old anger is boiling up inside of me, and I'm trying so hardest to hide it.

Mom's cocktail mask slips a little more, and I think she's going to break down and scream right there in front of everyone. "No, yeah. He never... He kept it inside. He kept it to...to himself."

Clara's mom nods and says, "What a shame, I'm so sorry, you should've been there, too"

I think Mom's going to cry. Instead, she holds her hand over her mouth. "I think," and she sighs, moves her hands, "I think I need to be excused for a few moments. If you don't mind?"

Before anyone could respond, she's up away from the table and walking out towards the garden. For a while no one talks, we're all silent. Then Clara's mom pipes up with cheery voice, all bell tones and harmony, "His poetry was really really very good. You guys should be proud. He could change the world with poems like those. He could change everything with his words."

Our sleeping bags are on the living room floor. Mom's upstairs sleeping in Clara's room. The skull sleeping bags look ominous to me. I remember the heads. The picture on the tablet is more real and poignant then even my memories.

I took a shower a little bit ago. My hair's still wet and my skin's a bit slick but I feel so much better than I have in a while. Clean.

That before smell was hard to scrub off, eventually replaced with odd perfume smells. I feel like I don't deserve to smell like that. Not with everything that's happened. Pretty things, nice things… They're for other people. They're for everyone else. People like Clara. Like her mom. Not people like me.

"My brother's poetry?"

Clara sits up. No lights are on. The only light we get is from streetlamps coming in through the blinds and moonlight. Maybe the bright flash of a car's headlights shining in and making everything more real. More physical. More human.

"What about his poetry?"

"Did you know about it?"

She's quiet. Car lights make the room brighter. Then dimmer again as they slide past.

"No. Mom went out by herself all the time."

"Herself?"

She's quiet again. And then her voice is sad, "Yeah."

I don't want to make the realization I do, but I can't help it.

"Where's...your dad? Where is he?"

Her words are bitter, anger on the verge of tears. That feeling is one I hold close inside and know all too well. "Just… Fuck. Just go to sleep, okay?"

I don't say anything. I know what she's going through. I've gone through it. It's happened over and over again. The strange tension in the air… I know that tension. I feel like everything is tight around me. Like I'm suffocating just thinking about it. I don't want that life for Clara. She shouldn't have that life.

"Do you want to do something?"

Clara's rolling over in her sleeping bag. I can watch her in the shadows. "Like what?"

"Do you have any more cheap wine?"

She laughs. "I guess. Why?"

"We should go on another adventure. Not anywhere near the midway, though."

"Yeah, fuck that place. What's your plan?"

I kick the sleeping bag off my body, off my legs, like I was crawling out of a body bag. "That school. You still think that's safe?"

"Yeah, let's go and do that. I need to get the fuck out of here."

I stand up. "Good. Now, what about that cheap wine? You still got some?"

She grabs my arm, leading me to the kitchen. "My mom's got a huge stash of it in the basement. She drinks it when she thinks no one's looking."

We slowly open the door, flick on the light and go down. At the bottom of the stairs, I noticed that the walls are covered in poetry, pasted like wallpaper. Some are written in scrawled handwriting, others are cut out from magazines like ransom notes. Clara doesn't seem to notice it at all, so I try and pay it no mind. Even though it feels weird, and creepy and not right. Was this her mom's poetry? Was it her poetry? I don't know. Maybe I don't want to know. One of the lines repeated over and over again involve biting the sun and devouring the moon, and I feel sick to my stomach. I just want to get the wine and get out of here already.

We're back in the garden in the broken-down high school. We're drunk again, and laughing. The moon looks the same as the other night.

Clara's in a tree now, hung upside down. Her hair is around her head like a halo. "Look at me! I'm a tarot card!"

And we both laugh for a moment.

"You should probably stop that."

"What? Why?"

"Cause you're drunk."

"No," she giggles. "No, you're drunk."

"Yes, Yes I am. But I'm not hanging by my knees from a rotting tree."

She climbs back up. In the moonlight, she looks sober and sad all of a sudden. "Oh. I don't like this tree anymore." She starts scaling down the tree.

"Why not?"

She gets down, sits in the grass with me. We don't need our flashlights right now. The moon is bright like a living light in the sky. It shouts out the shadows with its voice. "Why not what? Oh, right!" More giggles. "This fucking tree. Fuck. Tree. Fucking tree. I was hung on it, like draped on it. Like a dead snake."

Shit. "You did have that dream."

"Duh. What? You think I'm fucking with you?"

"No."

"I mean, I said that."

"Yes, yes you did. I don't know. It's different now."

"How?"

I laugh because I have no idea what I mean. Something good? I know that much. But beyond that? I don't know.

Clara smiles and says, "Hey, I got it."

"What?"

"Why don't we… Fuck. Why don't we…? Fuck. Let's go look at the art."

I smile and agree because I like the graffiti they've got on the walls. Who doesn't love it? I even think about my phone and maybe taking pictures this time. It's a cheap phone so the pictures might not come out the best, but it's something.

So, we go run through the halls.

We still pass that jug. I can't feel my lips. We're taking pictures and the pictures are moving and it makes me laugh. Last, we come to that giant human body spray paint. It doesn't look like a real body. It's like some old medieval concept of the body. Parts are all symbolic animals. The lion where the brain should be. Lungs are snakes. A bird for a heart. "Does this look different to you?"

Clara says, "No. It's always looked like this?"

And I show her the picture from the other day.

"Oh, that's before my mom fixed it."

"What?"

Clara doesn't respond. She's crawling away. I hear strange sounds and I follow her, follow her body and we crawl, both of us. I feel like I'm going to throw up, but I don't want to be alone in these halls. I don't know what's crawling through these halls.

She leads me to the garden again and everything is different. The moon is gone. The tree is covered in dead snakes. I vomit and then try and run, but everything spins. And then oh shit, I'm out and on the ground before I know it.

When I come to, I don't remember anything from last night. I'm flooded by these random images. We're not in the garden or anything like that. Not anymore. We're back in the house, in the slumber party living room. Popcorn is scattered on the floor and Clara's still asleep. She doesn't look real, the way she sleeps there. She looks like a doll.

I remember the dead snake tree from my dream. And I remember a little girl trapped in a large crystal. Something about her made me so sad, and it carried over into my waking hours. That heavy sadness in my heart, and I felt like I knew here, but couldn't place how or why. Had she been at the Safe House? No, I would've remembered that. And there was this shadow, an old scarred man. His clothes were rags and he was covered in tattoos of what looked like poetry. I remember being so terrified in the dream, and the fear woke me up. My heart pounding, my body coated in a cool sweat all clammy. Breathless, like I'd been running in my sleep.

I sit up, my head fuzzy from just waking up, and for a moment I think I see Allison's ghost in the corner of the room. Her wheelchair squeaking as it moves towards me, her eyes intense, serious. She is trying to warn me of something, but I have no idea what. And then, just as quickly, she's gone.

Clara's mom walks into the living room. She's holding the empty jug. "Look what I found. You girls had a lot of fun last night, didn't you?"

My face is red and on fire.

I don't know what to say. I am so numb right now, and I never thought I would miss that animal pain inside of me, and the need to cut it out. But here it is, that numb broken feeling making me lost and adrift and missing that painful part of me that felt something, anything at all. Even if was a jagged edge of a broken bottle against my arm.

"That's okay. We had fun too. Sometimes you need to have fun, right? Especially if the world's ending and we're all fucked anyway."

Then she sees the look on my face. And it's like, she changes.

Right then, right there. Like she had forgotten for a moment who she was pretending to be and slipped, and showed the real person under those walls of her perfect suburban mask.

Her voice becomes chipper. "Anyway. Your mom's sleeping it off just like my little Clara there. Do you want blueberry muffins? I have some here. They're my cheat every morning. I'm not supposed to eat them, but I don't care. Besides, do I look fat to you? No. No, I don't. I look fan-tas-tic. So, if I eat a muffin a day, who cares? Right? Yes. Who cares. Muffin?"

My head hurts and my mouth tastes like acid and rainwater. The numbness is still there, but with a sense of danger on the edge of it. Like I know this is all wrong, that a distant part of me is screaming in warning? But it is so far away, I can barely sense it over the numb waves inside of me. "No, no thank you. I'm not...I think food is bad right now."

"Oh, of course honey. I'm so sorry. Coffee? I grind it myself and use a French Press. It makes the best taste, you know? And don't worry: I only use fair trade beans. There will be no blood in my coffee. No blood for my coffee at all."

"Yes. Coffee sounds nice. Thank you," I say and I look at Clara.

She reminds me of my brother. Sleeping still, not moving. I want to go over and put my hand on her chest. See if she's still breathing. She can't be like him. I should try and visit him today.

I think about looking at my phone for photographic evidence of what exactly we saw and what was just some dream image in my head. I decide not right now. Looking right now would be bad. I can't see the truth by myself. It is too early in the day for truth.

Clara's mom takes us to school while my mom decides on sleeping in. And I let her; she needs this. Clara's got dark sunglasses on like some cartoon hangover character. Her mom's being chatty but I barely hear her. All I can think of is my brother, carted off to some Sleep Room, whatever the fuck that was. And I have to go to school now. Because I have no other choice.

Maybe I can skip some classes. Run out for a bit. Get away.

I don't know.

I want to see my brother again.

I hold myself. Clara's mom drones on and on... I can't hear her. It's like a monotonous low hum.

`The school day is a numb fog.` I don't want to be here. I know they don't want me here. I make people feel uncomfortable. I can see it in their eyes.

People keep walking up to me to say they're sorry. Saying my family is in their thoughts. I don't want to be in their thoughts. How do I know what they're thinking of? Keep me out of your fucking thoughts. I can barely live in my own thoughts. My own thoughts are bad enough as it is.

I'm sleep walking from class to class. I see Clara later in the day and I'm so glad. She treats me like I'm human. Like I'm existing and bad shit happens and that's it. Bad shit happens to people and it doesn't mean we treat them like strangers. She gets that. She says "I think our parents had too much fun last night."

And I reply with a solemn, "Yeah, guess so."

"It's good for my mom, you know? She's. Well, it's rough for her right now."

I pull my book bag over my shoulder. The hall is crowded. I feel like a fish trying to swim through a busy current of people. "Oh? Yeah?"

"Yeah. She needs something other than..."

"Then what?"

"Nothing."

She walks quickly between the people to get away from me. She doesn't want to answer that. I don't know why, I don't care either way. Whatever she says can't be as fucked up as what's going on with my family lately. My family are the kings and queens of fucked up shit. Although I will say it was weird waking up in that house with everyone hungover. But what is normal? It's all fucked up. We're all fucked and fucked up.

Come to think of it, I've never seen Clara's dad anywhere. I know he exists. There all these pictures of him everywhere. I just don't know how real he is anymore.

I think about Clara's mom desperately clinging onto this concept of suburban bliss. It's a damaging idea. It's like, what? Utopia. Shangri-la. Neverland. Narnia. I would say Wonderland, but that shit's fucked up and dangerous. Maybe that's it. Maybe her mom's clinging onto this Narnia of a life, even though she's seen the Wonderland beneath it all. Once that Cheshire gets into your head, it never goes away. The cracks start to show through.

I feel bad for them. For Clara. It's not a superiority feeling, knowing that they're seeing what everyone else without blinders sees now. It's a sadness, like somehow their innocence is loss. Like the moment when you're a teen and you realize that your toys don't have meaning anymore. I remember that feeling, that loss. Like all your friends are dead and you can never go home again. Before the campground fire, I had nights I was up trying to play with those toys, trying to remember what it was like, trying to reconnect to that world again that world I lost.

But now those toys are burned up in some stupid fucking fire.

At lunch, I see Rowan and his group. A combination of all genders milling about him as he sits on the orange plastic table. When he sees me, he smiles and motions for me to come over. I walk over to him and he points for me to sit down. I shake my head no.

"What do you want?" I say. When I speak my words, have gravity to them.

"To give you my love."

"Shut up."

He laughs. "Dylan won't be bugging you again."

I am shocked and I stand rigid still. I can sense murder in the air; it smells like blood. "What do you mean?"

"He was a good poet, but he broke everything apart. He ran away from us. He knows he can't do that. He knows that our art is more important. It's way more important than any little crush he might have. Fuck him. You'll see soon enough. We have a new poet now and they are fantastic."

"Okay, um. Right." I turn to walk away, I don't want to be here anymore, I don't want to listen to this anymore. Everything spins and I feel itchy again, and the restless feeling inside of me. Fire. Needing to come out.

"Sorry about your campsite and all that."

I stop. "What?"

"It was a necessary thing. You'll understand and thank me someday."

I think of those toys burning up. My whole childhood burning up.

"What are you talking about? I thought Dylan did it?"

He gets off of the table. I hear his followers all clamoring around him like a swarm. "What the fuck? What? Were you there? Were you? No. You can't give Dylan credit for that! You can't call us a bunch of plagiarists. We don't fucking plagiarize! You can't do this to us! It is our poem! Our gift to the world!"

16

They close down the school when I find Dylan's body on fire in the girl's bathroom.

I didn't want to—fuck—I didn't want…

Fuck! I am so sick of death, so sick of seeing death. Fuck. Why did *I* have to be the one who found him?

Rowan.

That fucking asshole.

They'd strung his body up between the stalls. The door had been removed and placed on the floor to catch his blood. Blood on blue paint. His arms were tied to the edges of the bathroom stall. Spread out. His chest was open, ribs pried apart. They look like fingers on hands. Crows in his chest. They fluttered in the air, their feathers falling around the body, black feathers falling on blood falling on blue paint. The afternoon light came in through the slats on the windows. Beams of light, falling on the body. Shadows of birds falling on the body.

On the floor were five headless bodies. Dismembered. Placed in a spiral, their spines twisted in unreal positions. I felt an emptiness and overwhelming beauty when I saw all of it. And sadness.

Dylan and I had problems, yes. But they were just that. Stupid fucking problems. Death wouldn't solve them. Even a death like this.

I was curious. I was in shock. I was so many things. I went up, put my hands on his face. I leaned up and kissed his lips. The kiss of the living to the dead, a goodbye kiss.

When I kissed him, the cuts on my arm felt like someone was pushing tiny needles into them. I was dizzy with pain. I stepped back. Dizzy. Overwhelmed with pain.

Then Dylan's body caught fire. The lips first, then the head.

My pain subsided then.

I stepped out into the hallway, stepped out in shock. Smoke billowed out from it. Everyone whispered. Moved away. Moved from the door. The fire alarms sound like air raid sirens. People stopped whispering, some screamed, pointed at the smoke. The heat grew in the air, hungry, as everyone ran around me. I felt like I was swimming upstream, pushing my way through the panic. I didn't run at all. I just walked. Cautiously, carefully. I walked to the office. To see the principal. To let him know his school was burning down and there was poetry all over the bathroom walls.

The principal didn't even want to see me. Even when I told him what I saw, what happened. He thought I was insane. He thought my coma brother and missing father and homeless family had made me completely bonkers. That I was making shit up. Even with the air raid sirens going on and on. Even with the students filing out. When he found out that there was death, really death and fire and everything was burning up, he yelled at me. He thought I did it.

Of course, when they used fire extinguishers to put it out, to pull the body down, to give it an autopsy, that was when they knew it wasn't me. They wanted the body to speak. They wanted to hear the words come out of burnt lips. What would it whisper? They wanted to know. They wondered.

Autopsies and times of death and they knew that I was in class. That they all had seen me. They knew it wasn't me. That it couldn't have been me. Too many eyes. Too eyes many seeing me. Speaking to me.

Part of me thinks of telling them about Rowan. About all I knew.

I'm not stupid. I watched the cops bungle around my brother. I watched them mess up again and again. They never found him. They never found who did this to him. They never found anything. Not even the severed heads, they didn't find it. I did.

I'm not going to tell the cops shit.

It's time for me and Clara to step up our Nancy Drew routine.

It's time to fix this ourselves.

It's time to put this fire inside to a good use.

I wait outside as sirens are yelling *fire, fire, danger, fire*. And I hear the ambulances now. And the fire engines. I see them pulling up. Smoke pours out of the building and the fire inside of me is quiet now. Did I let it out again? Was any of this real, really happening? Did my kiss set Dylan aflame?

People walk past and most of them ignore me. Not even turning a head as I stand by the tree by the library. I look for Rowan. I look for any of his friends. I don't see them. I wait and wait and I don't see them.

Eventually, Clara comes up and stands next to me. We're both looking at the smoke. At the firemen barging in. At the cops pulling up. I know that they need to put that fire out, find the body, find out I am innocent. But I want the fire to thrive. Putting it out would be killing some part of me. I couldn't watch that. I couldn't watch them killing some part of me.

"Let's go," I say to Clara.

Neither of us speak. We walk in silence

"My mom's not picking up her phone. Can your mom come pick us up?" I say, as I look off ahead into the sun. I can't look behind. Looking behind will turn me into salt.

Clara sighs. "No. I can't call her at work."

"Oh. Now what?"

There are no words for any of this. Feelings can't become words. Words are failing, flailing. Every word that comes out of my mouth is the wrong word. It's like the minute it hits my lips it becomes something else. Something full of lightning and laughter.

"Let's try and see my brother."

"Oh, okay."

And that's that. It's settled then.

Fuck the cops. Fuck the hospital. Fuck everything. I'm going to see him. I'm going to see my brother.

"We can't let you into the Sleep Room."

Nurses, doctors, security guards. We keep asking because I can't stop. We ask everyone we can. Finally, someone hands us a newspaper. It's a weird thing to touch a newspaper. I don't think I've ever used one, not even going to the local news website or anything. It feels so strange. Like I'm walking through some different era. I want to google this newspaper now.

On the front cover? Ten missing teenagers found.

"So?" I say. She acted like this was supposed to explain everything.

"It means your brother isn't the only one in the sleep room now. It also means that we're really busy right now. Okay? We don't have time to help you out at all. We're preparing beds; we're getting the equipment all set up. We're going to be busy. So, it's probably better if you just leave, okay? Just go and come back later."

"Come on." Clara pulls my arm, yanks me towards the back. "Let's go."

I resign myself to her movement. I let her pull me, yank me, take me elsewhere. I want to go home now. Where is home? I feel so lost and abandoned and drowning and on fire and all this shit…

Inside I'm yelling and screaming, but outside? I don't know. I have this weird calm.

"Can we talk?"

Clara looks right into my eyes. Her eyes are so big. Brown. I don't think I've seen her small freckles until now. They're like a mirror of my freckles. Are we mirrors of each other? Would I have had her life if mine hadn't fallen apart? If I had been an only child? Did I really want her life?

"Talk about what?"

We're wandering around the streets, waiting for one of our moms to come and get us. We've been in the library, been in coffee shops, went to the parks, sat on benches. Watched the lake water turn into waves.

"What you saw. What did you see?"

"Dylan. Fuck. Dylan."

"Did you? I mean, was he on fire?"

I stop walking, my legs weak and I can barely stand. I reach out with my last bit of strength and hold onto the wall, every muscle shaking with tiny tremors. All of my energy was gone, spent. Even remembering it now, thinking about it now, brought the cuts on my arm to life, my hair standing up on end, the fire inside wrapping around my bones. I touch my lips and they burned from that kiss.

"Not right away. There was like...his ribs were full of birds. And the heads we found? I think the bodies were there, torn apart and arranged."

And then Clara leans in, leans in close.

I'm still dizzy, still disoriented, I can barely think straight. Every time I try and concentrate on what I saw, my body trembles and my lips and cuts burn and I feel so overwhelmed.

Her face is so close to my face, her eyes big, moon eyes. Her pupils seem dilated, her lips trembling a little. She twists her shirt with her fingers, and her eyes are probing me, searching for something under my skin.

"How does it make you feel?"

I think I'm going to vomit. "What the hell is that supposed to mean?"

Clara moves back, like I was a viper ready to lash out. "Nothing."

Her movement is nervous, like she wants to stop talking, but I can't just let it slide. After everything I've been through, after everything we've seen together, how dare she ask that?

I want to scream at her. She was my friend, what the hell happened?

I am just done with all of this. Done with everything. How was I able to start that fire? Why was Dylan there? Everything inside of me is so broken. I am so hurt and exhausted and emotionally wrung out.

"No. You don't get to say nothing after asking a question like that. What do you mean by how does it make me feel? How did seeing all those severed heads make you feel? Fuck. Fucking hell."

She's hiding her face under her hair, backing away from me. I've never seen Clara act like this before: nervous. She was always the proud one, the one ready to fight and stand up for everything. So smart, so beautiful, so on top of everything. But now, now, not in this moment. She was terrified, like someone opening night right before a play, or how I felt in art class when the teacher graded my final painting and found it lacking. "Look, it doesn't matter, I guess. I mean. Maybe. Still. Was it beautiful? I need to know, you have to tell me, please."

Still dizzy, still trying to keep myself together, limbs still trembling. I feel that fire on the edges of my body and I want to welcome it back into this world. I think about it, and yes, holy shit. It was beautiful, wasn't it? I hate myself for thinking this, but it was.

"Yes," I say, against my better wishes. "It was beautiful."

And I want to cry.

Now Clara moves in a little closer to me, whispers to me, and I shiver. "Did you set the fire?"

I shake my head. I don't want to tell her the truth; the truth makes no sense at all. "No, I don't know. No. I don't think so."

"That's a nice touch though, don't you think? The fire."

I want to nod and agree with her, because it was a nice touch. It was my touch. My flame. My devouring light. Something sparked inside of me, and I had to, I had to let it...

Clara chews on her tongue. She holds her phone to her face. "Shit, I got a text from my mom."

"I didn't hear..."

"She's said we should go to the park and wait for her there. She'll be along shortly."

"Oh, okay."

We turn around and start walking back. I go slowly, still woozy, my legs a little less wobbly. "What did you mean? By all that? A nice touch? The body being beautiful?"

Clara's walking fast, head down, her body shrinking in on itself. She was a shell. She had her defenses up. She did not want to talk.

I want to hold her or have her hold me or something. I want my friend back. What was going on? She was acting so weird. She felt fake, like she was made of plastic.

"You need to talk to Mom."

"I do?"

"Yeah, you do."

I keep trying to talk about it, to see what she meant, and she kept saying I need to talk to her mom. That I had to talk to her mom. That this needed to wait until her mom was here.

The ride back from the police station is silent.
I felt like I was in custody forever, with interview after interview after interview, repeating my answers into numb submission.

Both moms are in the front seat. My mom has borrowed some of Clara's mom's clothes. They look like twins. All dressed alike. The same shoes, shirts, pants….

We're all quiet. It's like something is happening, we can all feel it but we can't speak about it. We just let it happen around us. Speaking about it won't stop it from happening and there is no way to stop it anymore. Whatever this is. Whatever we're becoming.

A family of some kind? A broken thing?

When we pull into the driveway, we sit for a second. Doors locked tight. I want to get out, but we sit in silence. At first I think, who died? And then I think: Dylan. And the others. And I found them.

I want to vomit. Maybe I'll feel better if I vomit. I'll feel clean inside. I want to be clean. I'm so full of all this noise and fire and light. The fire is back inside of me again. That fire at the school wasn't enough. I guess it will never be enough.

I am the fire the fire, the fire…

I am the fire.

Fire.

"It's hard. I know that. It's been so hard on you," my mom's talking, "You shouldn't have had to see any of that, oh honey. I tried so hard to keep you safe from all of that, and it was no use. The world is such a horrible place, and I'm so sorry. You should have never gone to school today. I had this feeling something bad was going to happen and you should've just stayed with us, but it was just a feeling, you know? A silly gut feeling. I should've listened to it. I should've kept you here with us."

The fire courses through me, sings in my veins.

"I guess the school's probably closed now," I say, my words hoarse, my throat tainted with the smoke of my heart.

"Sort of," Clara's mom is talking, "They're renting trailers behind the school while they clean up all the debris and fix it all up. Clara, dear, you can stay home too."

We don't talk. I want to pry about the beauty of Dylan's death. But I don't want to ask Clara's mom in front of my mom. I don't want to drag her into whatever this is. She's been through so much lately, and I have a feeling I'm really far into it, deep down inside now.

"Is the hospital letting us see Casper at all? Are they still keeping him from us?"

Mom pops the locks and opens her door. "No. No visitors still." And her words are the storm.

"We're going to have a big slumber party tonight; I just talked to my mom." Clara's washing her hair in the bathroom and talking to me. I'm sitting outside, on the top of the steps. My mom's at the hospital trying to get in and see my brother. Trying to somehow infiltrate the Sleep Room. I wanted to go with her, but she said no and no again. I thought of sneaking into the car? But no. That wouldn't be right.

But I don't want to be here, either. Or anywhere either. I have this restless feeling. Every time I close my eyes, there is nothing but darkness. Then, all of a sudden, in that darkness is Dylan lit up on fire, his head like a lamp in my skull. Then I see the other heads, the ones from the other day, and they have candles in their skulls too. The flickering flames are lighting all that darkness in my skull

The restless feeling gets more restless. I have to keep moving, pacing. I need to cut again. The beast is inside me, screaming in the form of blood pumping, heart beating, fire blood, animal blood like a burning rhino trampling through my insides, screaming through my bones.

"Hazel? Can you hear me?"

I pretend to seem normal. Normal people aren't filled with all I saw.

She shuts off the faucet, pulls out her wet hair, wraps a towel around it.

"Mom had this idea, and your mom seemed to be cool with it. We think that all of this stuff is a lot for you, right? So maybe we would get a whole bunch of girls over tonight. Have a real sleep over? Maybe take your mind off things. Just be stupid fucking teenagers for once. Drink, laugh, play board games. Watch stupid horror movies."

"Okay."

I stand up, walk along the railing, looking down to the first floor. I see the living room: the couch, the chairs the television. It's laid out like a temple, I think. This is the place for prayers. The suburban altar. Clara walks up behind me. Touches me gently, like a touch of concern. Or maybe a touch of fear.

"Are you okay?"

"No, no."

"Right. Why would you be?"

My cuts scream.

"That fire, though. That was a nice touch. It was exactly what the poem needed. My mom was right, right? She knew you had it in you. She knew you could do it, make the poetry so fucking fantastic."

A sinking feeling in my stomach, the world feels so small and distant, like I'm viewing it from the bottom of a well.

I fucking scream, "What are you talking about?"

Everything is sliding into view. She kept asking if it was beautiful. What the poem needed. I feel this sinking sensation that I was truly alone now, that Clara was one of them, too. One of the murdering poets. And I remember the fire, the fire coming out of me, making my own poetry.

"Anyway, I was all broken up inside after we found those severed heads, right? And my mom: she said, it wasn't something to be sad about. She said that it was poetry. I didn't understand, you know? But then she took me into the basement, and she showed me all of her poetry. I never really paid attention to it before; it was just some weird wallpaper that grew over time covering the walls. I never paid attention to it, until my mom really showed it to me, explained it all to me. All of it. It was... I'll show you later. It was so beautiful. She was right." Clara puts her still damp hair in a ponytail and turns and looks at me. She's grinning, and it makes my skin crawl. She places both her hands on my shoulders, still damp, and I try to act normal, try to be normal. Is there any such thing as normal anymore? But I don't want her to see my reaction.

"Like the poetry of murder. I saw it. It made me weep. It was like...a religious experience. I'd never had one of those before." Her eyes are even bigger now, pupils dilated intensely, as if she's reliving that religious experience right now in this exact moment.

And I get chills.

"Never. Well, once. Do you remember? In art class. When we did the renaissance painters and all that. And they were all these images of torture and horror. Like the saints being hung upside down, or that one carrying her eyes on a platter. Those. I felt the same thing then, and I could see what my mom meant. I saw the beauty of the butterflies and the heads. I could see it! The poetry in shape and form."

I remember that day in class, I remember the look on Clara's face. It was embarrassing, like spying her most intimate moment in the world, and here it is again, looking at me in complete rapture.

I step back a little, carefully. The air is filled with dangerous vibrations and I just want to run. But I know running would be dangerous. This whole thing was just so dangerous.

My cuts start to whisper beneath the scars in the voice of fire…

"And my mom showed me the photos of when she went with Rowan and those other kids from school, to do this poetry reading. It was like I found my home, my one true perfect home. And in that home? There were all these others who saw the beauty of it, too, just like I had. Others who probably had that same spiritual experience I had watching it."

My scars are burning up. My insides are howling. I feel like I have ghosts tied to every bone.

"And so…I wanted to write my own poem. My mom helped, you know. We had all these spare parts. And Dylan was ready. He understood. He was ready."

I look around. Can I run? I can't run.

Did Clara's mom also kidnap all of those kids?

Dylan. Clara killed Dylan. And her mom. Did they…? My brother? Did they…?

What do they have planned for me? Or for my mom?

And if they hadn't done that to my brother, if it was Rowan or someone else, did it matter? They were doing it. Someone, somewhere would be murder for words. Death for poetry.

I think she knows I'm being quiet. I need to talk. I need to talk to survive this. "Dylan was ready?"

"Yes, he understood. We gave him all the stuff he wanted, you know? Like right before hand, he couldn't feel a thing. He was the one who did that to his own ribcage. It was such an experience! Look at this, look at my arm!" I can see hair standing on end. "Look at that. Can't you feel it even as I talk about it? It's an electricity in the air. From my words, electricity. And you understand! You set him on fire. Oh fuck, I wish I would have thought of that! I wish I could have seen that. Mom was right: you're a true artist. Aren't you? A true artist."

She hugs me close then and I hug her back. I pretend to be loving. Emotional. When everything inside of me is a roman candle of rage and despair.

I get a message on my phone. It's from a number I don't recognize at all. At first, I plan on just deleting it. Spam. Crap. Just maybe junk maybe. I open it though. I'm curious.

Clara's downstairs getting the slumber party all ready. Unfurling skull sleeping bags. Popping popcorn on the stove. I'm still at the top of the steps. I don't want her to see it. Wherever it was from. Clara doesn't make me feel okay anymore. I feel wrong somehow. A different kind of wrong.

The text:

This is Stacey. Remember? Are you okay?

I pause. I glance through the balcony slats and see Clara running about. Getting it all ready.

No.

I wait. Why did she contact me? This felt odd. Then again, everything felt odd.

I'm not okay either, she sends back, *We're both haunted anyway. You can't be okay when you have ghosts inside of you.*

I bite my lip. It tastes strange. I check to make sure Clara can't see me as I text back.

How do you do it? I've tried everything. Even cutting them out. It only works for a little while. Then it all comes back. Screaming in my skin. They want to destroy me from the inside out...

I wait nervously for Stacey to respond. I keep watching Clara. I keep looking out for my mom or Clara's mom. I don't trust anyone. Not anymore. Not anything. They're all liars now. Every one of them. Full of lies like I'm full of fire.

You forgot already, haven't you? They don't want to destroy you. You can't destroy them. You need to change. You're lucky, your ghosts are a transformation. Mine are a suffocation.

I nervously think about a response. I want to see her again. But would it be safe now? Would any of it be safe now? I decide to do that later, to respond later. I save her contact info and then delete the conversations.

Do they know how I set the fire? Would that be something they would want for themselves? Maybe they wouldn't turn me into a poem. Maybe they would cut me open and use my blood for ink. Take that fire and transform it into the words of their choosing. Using the ghosts inside of me to make art out of others, murdering them with my blood. Abusing that light, that beast, that ghost. They would dry me of all my screams. Make me empty and spent of screaming.

What would be left?

An empty husk thing. Skin. They would leave the skin. Skin slack against what was left. I don't want my skin. They would leave me with only my skin. That would be it. Just me and my memories. I couldn't do that. I wouldn't let them do that.

This is my fire. These are my ghosts. This is my skin.

I am not a vehicle for poetry.

I am a burning song in the heart of the void.

My mom calls me.

"I still can't see him. Why are they doing this to us?"

"I don't know. I'm sorry, Mom, I don't know."

"I'll be back later, I guess. I heard there's some big slumber party?"

"Yeah, Clara's idea. She thinks it will help me?"

I don't tell my mom about the talk between me and Clara. I can't lay all of this on her, not after everything she's been through. It would absolutely crush her, and I have to figure out how to fix it myself. It's insane, but I have to do it. I have to protect my mom, even if that means I have to lie to her about everything for now. If I don't tell my mom...will she find out? Will she feel betrayed? By me? By Clara's mom? By everyone?

I feel betrayed. I feel betrayed by everything.

I feel betrayed by the trees and the sun and the sky. I feel betrayed by the clouds and the earth. I feel like everything is turning around, changing. The world is lying to me. Hiding secrets from me. Betraying me with shadows and light.

I feel betrayed by my own blood, my own skin, my own hair, lips, bone, fingers, tongue.

"You okay, honey? You still there?"

"Oh. Um. Yeah."

"Sorry, you were really quiet all of a sudden. I'll be back in a little bit. I'm going to try and see him again."

And then my mom's voice sounds strained.

"I just want to know he's okay."

"I know."

"I guess I'll be back soon. Let them know, okay? I don't want to miss the party."

And she laughs; a nervous broken thing. And I know how she feels.

I was really young. I don't remember how old. My mom used to sit with me on the ground and I'd tell her what to draw, and she would draw it for me. Unicorns, mermaids, pirate ships, dragons... whatever. I don't remember my brother being there. It was just me and her. Maybe he was small enough to be in a crib sleeping or something?

I remember how I felt. It must've been summer, the way the light came in. Just the two of us. I think about that time and I wonder what it would've been like if I'd been an only child. Would it have been so perfect? Would it had been always like that? How close would we have been...

But now? When I think about that? I think about how horrible it is now that my brother is gone from us. I can't help but think of life in reference to him. I guess having a younger brother does that to you. It frames everything as a binary. With two existences. With parallel realities. Two pieces of each other so close together...almost like twins. Taken from each part, each piece. Little bits and pieces of each other floating in the other. We're made of ether, I think. We're made of water and fire. We're constructed from primal things. We're made from each other.

The procession of SUVs start pulling in one right after the other. Lining the street. Girls in various pajamas come walking to the front door. Each carrying a different sleeping bag. I knew them all from high school pretty much. I wasn't friends with any of them. They were a different crowd. Normal, pretty makeup on plain faces. Lots of pink. Dancing to whatever popular thing was playing. They seem so...porous to me. Airy. Like you could breathe right through them. Human filters.

I didn't think Clara was friends with them either?

Maybe everything is different than I thought. Maybe I've stumbled onto some hidden reality no one told me about. Hell, I didn't even know these girls' names. I knew them as the others. The people walking around with vacant heads. Teenage girls who called their dads "daddy" and wore all the pretty dresses and were handed everything in life without even having to work for it. They didn't need to be smart or talented at all. They just had to exist and they were given everything. Girls we would frighten because it was fun to do it. Scream at them. Maybe toss worms near them and watch them squirm.

I know, it isn't their fault. I am where I am because of all these external circumstances. But then again, it is easy to blame them. To make them into effigies of my pain. I thought Clara understood. Maybe she did? Maybe she didn't? I guess I won't be burning any effigies tonight.

Clara's mom stands at the front door, welcoming them in. She's dressed in black with a mourner's veil covering her face.

Each girl that comes in kisses her finger tips.

I'm on the couch with Clara sitting next to me. The television is on with the sound off, some B-movie slasher thing. Purely grotesque. Blood and body parts and evisceration.

Clara's holding my hand. I want to ask her if she knew who these people are? How does she know them? But I see her smile and I know then. They are not her friends. They are here because her mom asked them to be here. They were here for Clara's mom.

Everything inside me is panicking, I feel the weight of the situation on my heart, like an elephant sitting on my chest. I am trying not to shake, trying so hard not to grasp for air or let them know the panic I feel inside. I want my mom to come home, soon, I need her to come home right now. The urge to cut is sliding into my thoughts again.

As the girls file in, they sit on the floor in a circle around the couch. They remind me of the heads: the heads in a circle.

Clara's mom closes the door behind us.

They all stare.

"Clara, Hazel: I want you to meet Susan, Susan, Susan, Susan and Susan. Susan and Susan here are twins."

They both wave hello.

"And the others you know from school? Isn't that right Susans? Yes. Of course, that's right."

Clara waves and she's eager.

I just stare. I don't think I ever noticed that they all had the same name before. It makes me feel like cutting myself again, feel that scream under skin, the blood mixed with fire.

They start giggling, and one of the Susans says, "Wow, I didn't know she was, like, your mom? Clara, you are so lucky to have a mom as artistic as she is. I mean, I don't even know what to say. I'm practically gushing! To be in her house! Her house! I am such a fan."

"Yeah, Susan's right," says another Susan. "We're, like, all huge fans of your mom's work."

Clara's mom blushes, but the humility is like something make believe. "Oh, girls. You are embarrassing me! Come on, let's start the movies. We have popcorn and brownies and other treats. And girls? We're getting pizza. Does that sound good?"

They all applaud.

I sit there looking at the living room, surrounded by Susans. I want to run. I want to set fire to everything. When one of the Susans raises her hand, I almost burst out laughing. I stop when I see how serious everyone is.

"Yes, Susan?" Clara's mom says.

"When is the sacrifice getting here? I can't wait to see you work."

I turn and look at Clara's mom. I don't want to be a part of this. Am I the sacrifice? Will it be my mom? Oh god, I hope my mom doesn't come home now. I have to find a way out. I need to leave right now.

"Let's worry about that later, shall we? For now, let's have a little fun. Who likes fun? Raise your hand, come on! Don't be shy! Hazel? Don't you like fun?"

I smile. It's a forced smile. "I guess?"

"Come on, this is all for you." Clara grabs my hand. Her smile is giant. "To help you. Cheer up!"

And I look around at all the smiling Susans.

I'm in the bathroom, trying not to talk too loud on the phone as I plot my escape. Originally, I wanted to wait for my mom, but now, I'm not sure waiting's a good idea. Something bad is going to happen. I don't want to be around here when it does. So much bad shit has already happened. I can't take anything more.

"Are you enjoying yourself at the slumber party?" Mom asks.

"I guess so? Are you coming back soon? It's getting. Well, weird."

"No," she says. "I can't leave without seeing him. I can't just give up on your brother, oh, I can't. He's still my little boy..."

"Clara's mom keeps asking about you? I guess she has a bottle of wine for the two of you to share while the rest of us girls play or something."

"Oh." I feel this strange apprehension in the air from her pause. "Her mom can be sweet. But she's...oh fuck. Hazel, can I be honest with you?"

"Um. Sure."

"Look. She's nice, but she's so overbearing. And she's so, so, so upper middle class. I can't be sucked back into that shit again, even if I am homeless."

Mom doesn't want to come here, doesn't want to save me. And I have to deal with all of this on my own, and my heart is struck with such sadness. It's overbearing, and I can't cut right now, but fuck it. I'm going to do something I haven't done in a long time.

I pull up my sleeve, and I dig my nails against my skin. The feeling sweet, the relief helping a little just a little, the scream dying back down.

Please, mommy, don't leave me to handle this all by myself.

"Is that why you're not here?"

"A part of it. I really do want to see your brother. But yeah, I guess that's part of it. It's too much being there. Too many bad memories from a time when I hated myself. Okay? I'm sorry."

"Then why do I have to be here?"

She pauses. Silence.

"I can't lose you too. As much as that place sucks ass, it's safe. Okay? It's safe."

"But Mom, it's not... It's not safe..."

"Don't argue with me, Hazel. Come and see me in the morning, okay? I'll be here unless they kick my ass out."

And then before I can say anything, my mom hangs up on me. And I have to do everything I can not to cry out, not to collapse into a pile of shaking limbs and anger.

I try and call her back, again and again and again. Nothing; mom's no longer answering and I bite the scream down and the pain helps a little, just a little. So, I start digging my nails into my arm again, sharp and the anger abides a little, just a little, but not enough. Why would my mom abandon me like this?

Something moves again under my skin. The memory of fire is alive inside of me. I need to set the fire free. Just scratching isn't enough anymore. I need to cut; I have no more blood. I am filled with fire. And I am so angry at Clara and her mom. So angry at everything they did. What they did to my brother. What they're going to do tonight. Everything they did to my family. This anger is a fire inside of me. I need to set it free.

I look around in the bathroom. I open cupboards. I find a box of spare safety razors and I pull one out. I take my other arm, hold it out.

One. Two. Three.

I cut. Hold my breath. The pain is only there for a moment. Once it's gone, I feel better. I exhale. I'm emptier now somehow, but empty is good. I need to be empty now. Empty is a void. No longer bones screaming.

I touch my finger to the mirror and my cut itches a little. And then, the mirror fogs up and I see nothing but flames where my head should be.

I open the door. I walk outside. I forget that my arm is bleeding. I don't fucking care. Fuck it. I don't need to clean it up. I just need to smile and let myself burn.

19

"Hazel? Hazel..."

Clara stands there looking at me in the upstairs hallway.

My head feels so hot. My cut itches and I look down. I see more cuts than I remember...many more. Crisscrossing my arms and legs.

I smile at Clara. I burn at her. "What? What's wrong, Clara?"

I pretend like I'm normal Hazel but I can't be normal anymore. I want to burn them all down. What they fucking did. What they all fucking did.

My brother.

My little brother.

My baby brother.

Hiding from storms, scared of thunder and lightning. Hiding under blankets and me comforting him. Sure, that was so long ago, but they put all that in a box and locked it away. Now, he sleeps. They all sleep.

Clara and her mom did that.

And Dylan. And the others. All the heads. All the bodies we found together. All filled with poems.

I hear Clara's voice cry out, "Um... Mom? Susan? Someone?" And she sounds so scared and alone.

Maybe there was a part of me, long ago, that would've felt pity for her. That would've somehow tried to save her. But not now. I am beyond all of that. I am the fire and the anger and I must destroy; it's as simple as that.

And so, I walk forward and stretch out my arms. I mirror Dylan's pose when I found him in the bathroom.

"What's a matter, Clara? You seem...perturbed."

There is a biting laughter at the edge of my words. Now the fire speaks for me, and it has a tinge of cruelty. Cat and mouse.

I hear the Susans cluster around the bottom of the stairs below. A murder of little girls all together like crows. Bird girls. All of them looking alike, acting alike.

I smile at them. The flames feel like hair. Like hair when you are underwater, and it's floating around you.

Clara walks a little bit backwards, step, step, step, clinging to the railing. She's looking for help. I don't see why. There is no such thing as help anymore. There is only the fire in the heart of the void. I thought she knew that. I thought they all understood that.

"This skin is so wrong," I say, "I want to take it off and let the fire breathe."

It feels so good to say that out loud for the first time. So, so fucking good. I feel my cheeks pinch from the pain of smiling wide. But it's okay, it's a good smile. It is the grin of truth.

As Clara moves back, I realize she's not afraid. I can see on her face that she's in awe. She is overcome with it. Her face looks holy. Pious. I remember what she said earlier about the beauty of death. About how she felt a religious experience with the bodies. With what they all call poetry.

"So, you want me to embrace you?" I ask.

Fire flows from my cuts. My skin is growing slack.

"Mom? Mom?"

Footsteps like anvils. She walks out of the kitchen and looks at us. In her hands are bowls of popcorn. She looks right at me, looks through me like I am invisible. Like I am cellophane.

My fire burns stronger. Burns brighter. My fire is like the sun's fire.

Clara's mom sets the popcorn down and looks at her daughter.

"Come to me," and Clara runs down the stairs. She runs to her mom and hugs her and I hear her crying.

"Hazel," her mom utters. "I knew you were a natural. When I saw you, I just...I knew it. You had this poetry yelling at me from the back of your eyes. You are so raw with talent. I can help you. I can help you focus this fire and transcend it all. Don't you want to be something greater? Don't you want to be a nova instead of a sun? Why just burn when you can take whole worlds out with you? Come here. Come to me."

My skin is so loose. I want to just slide out of it. Let the fire breathe. I walk towards the banister and lean over it. I think of jumping, being a burning light in the air. Maybe crawling on the ceiling will spread my fire, spread it over all of them.

I need to die now, die now and then become something other... Maybe just light. Maybe just fire and nothing else...

I want to see if I can float. Maybe I can. Maybe I can. Maybe I am without gravity. Maybe I can float. Maybe I can...

I am about tell her NO. I want to tell her to fuck off. All of them to just fuck off. But they stare at me and everything feels so dangerous. I am completely overwhelmed by the roaring sea of flame inside of me, and for a brief moment, it terrifies me. What gave me power now feels so dangerous, so destructive, I worry it will destroy me as well. That every last part of me will explode in a wave of fire and light, and all that will remain of me will be a pile of bones and ashes and nothing else. It shakes me to my core, and my heart pounds, and I feel fear stronger and greater than anything else. I fear this fire inside of me, and the awesome power it holds.

I am nuclear reactor on the verge of meltdown. Instead, I let my fire cool a little, tighten my skin. Blood still pours from me in rivers over my skin. I don't care. My head feels less hot and my hair is just hair again. The terror of my own fire recedes a little, and then a little more. Like waves on the beach, receding.

I tilt my head down, my hair in front of my eyes. I don't say yes. I don't say no. I have to play this close. I need to survive the night and then I can figure out what to do next. This is a dangerous place. I know I am in danger.

They killed their own. Dylan was one of them. The missing teens? Probably also connected to them. And my brother? My fucking *brother*? I feel a flickering again and shrug it off.

I walk down the steps and she's holding her hand out. I see it but don't take it.

She says, "Oh, my little girl, you made the right choice. It was the perfect choice. Your poetry will devour the world. Swallow everything whole and leave us with darkness."

The Susans are agasp and staring. I have no words for any of them.

Clara's eyes are a mix of awe and jealousy.

Her mom. I see it now. She's jealous of how her mom's treating me.

I am in the wasp's nest.

"Now, do you know when your mom's getting here?" Clara's mom asks. "Everything will really start then, you'll see. That's when transcendence will be reached and you'll see the meaning behind everything. Every rock, every speck of dirt, this table, this chair… even this popcorn. It all has a hidden fire.

"You've seen it? You've seen it. We will make it visible. And you, you my dear…" She walks up and Clara's jealousy in the air is thick like a fog. "You are the key. Your poetry will take us out of the cave; it will crush our chains. There will be no more shadows, only the fire in your heart. That is your poem, and tonight? Tonight is the first step."

I feel the flames licking at my insides again, wanting to roar and devour and destroy. I feel the anger and the terror at what I'm capable of, and part of me wants to give into it, to let it subsume me and devour the world. But then I picture my mom and my brother and I think no, not yet. Not until I know I can keep them safe. Not until I know that it won't be the death of everything. My heart is an atom bomb.

"Come on, tell us. When is your mom getting here?"

Oh no, this sinking feeling rises up inside of me like vomit, a feeling that they're all going to kill my mom, and they want me to be a key part of it somehow. And I won't. Fuck it. I won't ever let that happen. Fuck their poetry. Fuck their art. They will not use my fire like this; I cannot let them.

"Later?"

Clara's mom claps and then says, "Well, that will be later then, won't it? Come on, girls! Let's have some fun. The pizza will be here soon, we have popcorn, we have movies! Let's do this right. We don't want her to be suspicious, do we?"

My body is burning up again, the flames more powerful, the need to devour the world spinning around inside of me. I am terrified of this, and I look around and see the greedy look in their eyes, the want and the need. They see what I am, and what I've become, and they are pushing me further and further.

I cannot be around them anymore, not without exploding. And I didn't want to die, not yet. The world is pain, the world is suffering, but I had to keep going. My fire is both my life force and somehow the destructive passion of living all rolled up into a single, combustible death-drive. If I stay here any longer... God. That would be it. That would be the end of all and everything.

Shivers in my spine. The fire so strong, so terrifying. Everything inside of me clenched tight in fear, my heart racing. Have you ever been close to a house fire, or a car fire, or forest fire? That elemental heat singing your skin, and it is so beautiful, you want to join it. But also, so terrifying and overwhelming. That was my blood, that was my heart.

I had to leave. Oh god. I had to leave now.

I want to call my mom so she can hear the sad panic in my voice and know that something is wrong. That everything is wrong. Maybe this time she'll actually listen to me, if she thinks I'm in danger. I hope so, oh I really hope so. But I also don't want them to overhear what I'm saying. A text is probably the best idea.

I'm in the bathroom, kneeling on the floor. It must look like I'm praying. The phone is in my clasped hands; my head is bowed. I need to do this. I need to figure this out.

I hold my breath, count to three. The fire is growing inside of me, and I need to get out, I need to stop. I want to cut off all of my skin. I want to burn so bright. But I need to hold this in. How can I control this? I need to find a way to focus the fire, like a poet controls the line of a poem. It has to work for me, do as I say, and not explode in a billion rays of light.

Listen to me fire, listen to my breathing. In out, in out, like waves of the sea.

The way Clara's mom looked at me earlier… It was a hungry look. She wants this fire. She wants to use the fire inside of me. That is all I am to them. A tool. A quill. I will not let them control me, and have me explode for their purpose. I am not the poem; I am the poet.

Breathe some more, come on fire, listen to it, the slow symphony of my lungs. Listen and obey my song.

I open my eyes. I exhale. I quickly type on the virtual keyboard: *Do not come here. Whatever you do, do not come here. Stay at the hospital, or in the car, or something. Do not come here.*

And I'm thinking *please, please don't. Please just let this all happen and if I survive the night… Oh damn. I need to survive the night.*

Someone knocks on the door.

"You okay?" Clara's voice. It sounds anxious.

My phone vibrates.

"Yeah, um. Just a minute."

I check and my mom texted back already.

Everything all right?

No, no it's not. Nothing is right anymore.

We sit in the bathroom and talk. "Do you remember the first time we stole my mom's wine? We hung out in this same place, drinking and talking about stupid shit."

I nod. "I remember. We got so fucking drunk so fucking fast."

"I think you puked in the bathtub, remember?" Clara laughs. "And we had no idea what to do. We were like tripping all around and worried we were going to get caught."

"Yeah." I take another swig. "Do you remember when you wanted to spend the night at my house?"

"Right. I found out you were homeless then."

We were both silent.

Knock knock knock.

"FUCK OFF!"

I roll these thoughts around in my head as I drink. I feel fuzzy and everything's okay. Clara's being Clara again. And this whole poetry shit with her mom? It's probably nothing. I'm calm and washed clean by warm waves of alcohol. I want to dunk down and drown in them. It wouldn't be like death anymore. Or nothing anymore. But instead like going to sleep, like being sucked back into the womb. The water is the birth of the world.

"I guess, I was embarrassed."

"Why? Hell hell hell.. Why? Why. Why?"

My anger starts roiling around inside of me, and I want to bite it back down. It is my fire; it will do what I say. But the fire wants to control me, to turn me into a pile of ash and rubble. And it sounds appealing, in a dark way, but I can't let it.

"Because… Look at your fucking house. It's perfect. Perfect family. All that shit. How could I compare? You had that life we all dream about. Happy families all living together in perfect harmony."

Clara hands me the flask and I finish it. Feel like warm all over and everything is funny. The tile feels smooth. I run my hands over it, push my face against it. I like the way it feels like tiny rain-washed stones against my cheek.

"Well, we know that's bullshit. My family was never perfect. All you saw was this fucking mask we all wore. And I'm so sick of masks. Everyone pretending. Putting on a good show. Fuck that."

"I wonder if it's all like that. You know? Happy smiling families hiding emptiness, some deep darkness that rolls around in them waiting for the lightning to come and open them up." I like those words. They seemed like perfect words.

"Not like this," Clara says. "Sure, Dad leaving us and all that? Yeah. But having a poet...and all of this. Fuck. All of this. I just...I don't know."

I nod. There is something still inside her, the Clara I knew and loved, my best friend through all those years. It was her mom manipulating her, I know that. I just want to save her, bring out still. Maybe I can. Maybe. "You don't have to do it? You know. You don't."

She pushes me and my face crams against the floor and it fucking hurts.

The fire is rolling again. That's what they want, isn't it? To give in. So beautiful. My cuts ache and I feel like I need to let it out, to let it all out. Maybe if I tear hard enough with my fingernails it would do the trick? Strip it clean, deglove myself with my own hands.

Clara's screaming at me, her face right next to my ear, the echo of her voice bouncing around in my head. "Fuck you. You think you can walk in here with your head on fire and be little miss perfect poet and then act like I can just walk away? Fuck you!"

And then she pulls me up, face to her face. Blood trickles down my cheek, and damn. That must've scraped my head? Oh damn. Everything is dizzy.

She's screaming even louder now, spittle from her lips flying in my face. "What do you want from us? Do you want to steal all of this from us? I told you how the poetry makes me feel. And for once? For once, she's not putting on a mask for me. It took her so long to show me her poetry, to show me her true self. Fuck you for acting like this is nothing."

"Right," I say. I feel queasy. The fire inside is making me sick. My bones tingling, my chest burning. The booze is fucking with it, fucking with me. Fuel for the fire. "Let's, um. Let's let one of the Susan's in."

I wanted to escape but I would have to sober up first. One of the Susans had to help me walk down the steps. I stumble and almost fall but she catches me. Clara needs help, too. And we see that the living room is changed. That everything is different.

The lights are off. Scattered candles give off a cold light, laid out in complex geometric patterns I can't even fathom. The Susans are perched inside the cage of candles. Clara's mom is sitting in the center of it all and she's nude, all of her skin showing. Her blonde hair obscuring her face but not as well as I would've liked.

Everything is moving, spinning… I feel sick and this doesn't feel real.

The Susans sit us down. They move me like I'm a puppet, and push me towards the middle. The booze is keeping me lopsided, sideways, not fully here. My fire is rumbling inside, a thunder of heat and lightning.

We're all quiet. The world is humming. Everything is alive. The minute I touch the ground, it feels alive, too, like a breathing thing. The candles are the same: dripping, living flame. Everything feels so alive, always in motion.

Clara's mom looks at me. "When is your mom getting here?"

I check my texts.

You're in trouble? Fuck. Coming back.

I want to tell her no, don't come back, but the whole room is spinning and I want sleep to come but maybe they'll slit my throat in my sleep and pour the fire from my neck into gold cups.

"I don't know," I say and it's somewhat honest, "They're still not letting her in to the room. The Sleep Room? So, she's still trying."

Clara's mom nods, claps her hands. "The waiting is over. Let's move onto plan B. Is everyone ready?"

Humming starts from the girls. It moves with the breathing of the world. Everything moves with their song. Heartbeat. Breath beat. It's all alive. We're all alive.

Knives come out.

Fuck me. I don't have a knife? I don't like this.

They all open their eyes at the same time. Clara stands up, removing her shirt to reveal intricate paintings along her chest. Her ribs are covered in paintings of all these creatures in flight. Insects, birds, bats, all these flying things... Intricate designs. She points her head up to the sky, baring herself to the universe.

I see it in her eyes.

Clara is the sacrifice.

No. No. No.
Fuck no.
Not Clara.
Fuck no.

Her mom lunges.

Fuck no.

Fuck this.

Fuck no.

I love Clara too much even though she's lost and broken right now.

It's okay.

We're all lost and broken and searching for something and sometimes the wrong somethings come up, right? But right now, I'm not ready to lose another person I love.

Fucking hell, yes, I'm sober.
BAM.

The whole world gets clear. Everything is full of lightning.

I push Clara aside and the knife goes into me—a larger knife than I usually use. The pain washes in, and then the knife slips out when I exhale. My arm is slick with blood, but I don't scream. The pain releases me. And it itches. Fire shoots out of it, and I can't control it anymore. I can't focus it with my breath or my heartbeat. It just rushes out and I'm both relieved and terrified at the same time.

And her mom slashes at me, knife in the air, soaring at my face and just misses.

The fire is thirsty now, thirsty and ready to drink in the air and burn up everything.

Clara pushes me back, the fire dancing, as her mom swipes at her and tries to sink it in. The candles flicker around us, the fire calling to the fire inside of me. I don't know how much longer I can take before I explode and we're all sacrifices.

The Susans rise up, armed and ready to write their own poems.

I scream, "RUN!" at Clara and she seems to wake up. She grabs her shirt and we both take off into the garden. We don't even have time to close the doors behind; the Susans and her mom are running and screaming as we climb the fence and run out to the woods in the backyard.

The pine branches catch in our hair leaving needles and sap. Clara is crying and clutching her shirt to her chest. She doesn't have time to put it on; we don't have time to stop.

I can hear her mom behind us, her ragged breath haunting the air. Footsteps like soft echoes, and then she's there, behind us, diving into the shadows.

I almost lose control of the fire right there, as Clara's mom grabs her by her legs and she falls. The knife goes into her leg, into her back, into her neck. The sound is horrible, a jagged tearing noise.

I rush over and try to push Clara's mom off.

She stabs me. More pain. More release of fire and now…

Now…

Now I scream. This skin is a shell. I need to let it out. It is both terrifying and beautiful and amazing and I know this might be it, that it might just be the end of me and everything.

I shield Clara's body as she does her best to crawl away.

Her mom backs off, a smile on her face, knife in her hands.

The Susans surround me and cut in deep.

The pain overwhelms me. No release, no release, just pain, just pain and they cut like they are trying to carve holes in me, so they can shove birds in me…

Fire comes out instead. I keep them away from Clara's body as she crawls and crawls. A light from a car surrounds us in halos. I hear my mom's voice shouting that the cops are on their way.

Everyone scatters into the pines, their bodies becoming shadows.

Clara whimpers beneath me and I collapse.

My body is on fire when I collapse.

My body *is* fire when I collapse.

My skin is gone.

I am nothing but the flame.

Clara's dead.

They had a funeral for her and I couldn't go. Her mom would be there, and I couldn't play pretend and act like she isn't a fucking monster. My mom didn't go either. We wanted to so fucking badly, but these days? It's all about hiding in the pines and coming up with a way to expose the monsters. We need to expose the monsters. All of them. All of these fucking poets. The Susans, Clara's mom, Rowan and his gang of idiots. All of them.

My mom understood.

We sneaked into the funeral home the night before the service. Everything was dark. Everything was quiet. The night was bright with a full blaring moon, one of those moons that are as orange and almost as bright as the sun bright. It wasn't that hard to sneak in. Not as hard as we assumed it would all be. And we were silent. Our voices were caught in our lungs. And we saw her in the coffin.

Her face had cuts. And I think they must not have come and done her makeup or any of that yet? But she looked terrified. Her eyes were still open, her lips parted and letting her top teeth peek through. And the gashes… She was wearing a black princess dress. She did not look like she was just sleeping.

I wondered if her mom was mad that she wouldn't be poetry now.

Mad that we ruined all of this. Mad that she has a dead daughter on her hands, and a police investigation. No mention of poetry, though. Again, the cops and the detectives are all bumbling around her, bumping into clues and closing their eyes.

After we whispered our respects like prayers in the dark, we crawled back out through the basement window that we found earlier. We made our way back to the pines. We have one tent that was donated by some caring family and that's it. We both slept in there, and we had nightmares about everything. It was hard not to have nightmares.

We never talk about these nightmares. It's the one thing we don't share, we both know it would be too much. So, we keep the nightmares to ourselves, even though we are closer now than we'd been in a long, long time.

After school, I walk the winding walk through the pines, back to our new tent by myself. All of my friends were dead. It's a strange thing to think. All of my friends are dead. They were turned into poetry. And then I think: wait. No. Not exactly true. Stacey. Stacey is alive. Right?

As I walk, I listen to music and I text her at the same time.

Help me. Please, help me.

She doesn't respond right away but I don't blame her. How would I respond to the same text? I don't know. I've tried to save too many people and I've failed over and over again. I don't know if I had the strength in me to try and fail again.

I think...

I think...

I think the fire is gone. I'm numb now. I can't cut to feel it leave me. I can't burst with burning suns. Every attempt is a numb wave where the fire used to be. My skin is just my skin. My blood is like a low electric current flowing through me.

The fire, the fire.

I am empty now.

I am now.

The fire, the fire.

Some nights I dream of the heads full of butterflies. Other nights, I dream of Dylan. The only thing I never dream of directly is Clara. I dream of an empty coffin. I dream of being stabbed. I dream of her mom--maybe?--sometimes. But I never dream of Clara. I guess I can be thankful for that.

But inside of these other dreams, there is always water. Waves flowing over our bodies as we act and react to everything. Dark blue water, almost black and warm. A relaxation comes from the water, a light tingling. Not painful, but numbing. Calming. All my limbs numb.

It puts out the fire, I think. I dream only of water and the fire is gone. I'm not sure if I miss it. Maybe that's all a part of this. Of being numb? It's that I don't miss it. I want to miss it. But I don't.

Everything everything everything around me is
empty now.

I remember it before, when everything was full of fire and flames. When everything was moving and breathing. I remember feeling connected to the whole universe like it's some giant organism. But now this feeling is lost and gone and all that's left is numbness and emptiness. Sometimes I want to feel something, but I don't care enough to do anything about it. I don't even want to want it. I just have nothing. Nothing.

Why can't I have something?

But then again. Fuck it. I don't care. If I didn't have school, I wouldn't even get out of my sleeping bag in the morning. The hospital still isn't letting us into the Sleep Room. My mom goes to work and then goes there to watch over him.

There is numb ocean around us and we swim and sometimes we smile. I miss my mom. I miss myself. But I can't change it. I can't change anything. Everything is destroying us and we can't do anything about it.

And then Dad texts me. He doesn't even call. He just texts me.

Sorry about bro. Will come? Try. Try anyway. LU

I throw the cellphone against the high school bathroom wall. The screen cracks. For a moment, I felt something, and then it's gone like a flash of light in a storm. Here, gone. I caught the ghost of my being, a floating cloud inside myself. I want to reach out and grab it, but the water pushes me away, keeping me from being myself.

I don't respond to my dad. Fuck him.

DOESN'T MATTER THOUGH. Somehow, he finds out where we camped and his truck drives up. It's old and his favorite thing. Duct tape covers some parts of it.

When he gets out, I barely recognize him. His face is mostly beard. In the seat next to him are fast-food containers, wrinkled and balled-up letters and papers. My memories of him are clean-shaven, wearing a jumpsuit, smelling like beer. I remember him coming home, collapsing on the floor. Or sometimes friends dragging him to the house after a night at the bar, Him stumbling about telling us all he loves us or something like that.

This man? He is ragged and his clothes are patchwork things. He has a powerful frame. His gut is there, but it matches his body like a rock. Like a moving stone. When he sees us sitting around our campfire spot, he smiles. He walks towards us, cautiously. He holds out his arms like he wants a hug. But neither of us give him that satisfaction. So, instead, he sits down on a rock.

"Shit. Why so glum?"

Mom stands up, says sorry, and then goes into the tent.

"I know, I've been an asshole, but I needed to leave. I had to do it. You'll understand when you're older. Trust me! You'll understand. I know you will."

I don't say anything. I play with a stick for a few moments. Drawing spirals in the dirt.

"Clara's dead."

He holds his head down. "Oh. I'm so sorry to hear that. Was she your friend from, you know. The safe house? When you needed help?"

"No," I say. "No."

He thinks for a moment. Maybe Mom had a good idea. Maybe I should've just gone into the tent and ignored him.

"Clara, Clara. I think I remember her. Yeah. I think I do. I think you spent the night over there a few times. I remember her dad being a stuck-up shit for brains. And her mom? Oh, don't even get me started on that. She's something else."

I look at him. Really look at him. He seems so awkward around everything as if he doesn't know what his emotions are capable of. It seems so odd and wrong to see him like this. Like he's not my dad anymore. Like he's some stranger wearing my dad as a suit.

"She's dead. Clara's dead, Dad."

"Right." He rubs his beard. "Right. Yeah, maybe that's insensitive of me. I'm so sorry. I'm sorry your friend is dead."

"That's all right. You didn't kill her."

And then he stares at my arms. I pull down my sleeves and try to hide my cuts. I don't want him to see this; he has no right to see this. I feel vulnerable, like an egg ready to crack.

"What happened?" And looks at my neck. "Oh, honey what happened?"

He wasn't here. He's never here. I think he doesn't deserve to know. He doesn't get to play Dad when he feels like it's convenient for him. If he was here sometimes then maybe he would know all of this already. Instead, he's asking all of this and pretending to care. But when will he be back? And does he even have the right to care?

And so, I say, "It's nothing. Fuck it. Forget about it."

And he answers in a defeated voice, "Oh. Okay. I guess."

My mom still doesn't come out.

"Your brother," Dad asks.

"Yeah."

"What happened?"

Read the fucking texts I sent you. Read anything on the Internet about it. Is he this clueless? "He was missing for a while and when they found him, he was in a coma."

And he says "Oh."

"And there's this killing spree going on right now. Bodies turning up. All of them teenagers. And there are like ten of them still missing."

And he looks at me and says "Are you...are you...safe?" He's looking at my cuts, at my scars. Stares at them with worried eyes.

And I chuckle and say, "Fuck no. What the hell? Of course I'm not. My friends are being murdered and I found some of the bodies and... shit. Don't you read anything online? Any fucking news? Anything at all? Hell, listen to motherfucking NPR on the radio? What have you been doing?"

He shrugs, looks over at the top of the pines, his eyes ignoring mine. He wants to be invisible. I can tell.

"Living on a mountain. Watching for fires. Cut off from everything."

I hate that it feels good to see him again. I hate that I feel so betrayed, that he would rather be up on some shitty mountain watching for fire instead of being here, with me, his fucking daughter who was on fire all the time.

So, we sit for a moment more in silence. Then I go into the tent and sob in my mom's arms and try not to think about anything. Maybe I don't want to feel anything after all. Maybe I need to keep this numbness inside of me. Feeling shit hurts too much.

That asshole.

Eventually, Dad's head pushes between the tent flaps. His eyes searching at us. He seems lost. Jealous? Like maybe he wants to be a family again? But fuck him.

Mom turns her head; she can't even look at him. So, I guess it's up to me. I'm pissed at him for doing this to me. Making my mom feel so uncomfortable. Making me be the go-between.

"What?"

He looks at the ground, avoiding our glances. "Just. Hell. I'm going to go and try and see your brother."

Mom's still not looking or talking to him.

"Good luck," I say, "We haven't been able to see him for the past week."

He smiles. The fucker *smiles*. "I've got tricks, you know? Fuck. People *love* me. I bet I can charm them with a little bit of a smile and they'll let me in. Just you see."

And then my mom turns and looks right at him. "That's because they don't *know* you. Not everyone loves you. Some of us know the real you, know who you really are. Get out of this fucking tent. Go and pretend to be a dad for a few hours and then leave like you always do."

"Okay then. Nice seeing you too." Dad scrunches up his face, a look I've seen so many times before as a kid, growing up. Anger on the verge of tears. And then he moves his head out of the tent and slides the zipper up, in a quick, violent motion.

The air is stale in the small space. Mom starts sobbing and saying "that motherfucker" over and over again. We've been through too much, both of us, way too much. Him coming here, showing up? Trying to get brownie points for being a dad? That was something we did not need right now.

But he doesn't care. No matter what. He just does what he wants.

I don't know what to do. Mom's a mess. I can't talk to Clara. Clara's dead. I can't call Dylan. He's dead. I try and think of anything else. But nothing comes up. Maybe I should drift through this day like I drift through others? I don't know.

We needed to find out a way to prove her mom and Rowan and all of that were killing people. But...I just want to give up. Fuck it. Just give everything up.

Maybe I should go to Clara's house. Maybe if her ghost sees me, she'll just kill me.

Instead, I walk to the library. It's quiet. It's a place where people won't bug me, where people can leave me alone. I can read shit and be by myself. And I don't have to worry about people talking to me, wanting to see me, wanting to do anything.

The building is large and brick and old with stone lions are out front. I walk past them and go inside. The place is mostly empty with a few librarians and patrons walking around reading magazines. More on the second floor on computers.

I walk past newspapers scattered on wooden tables. Big front-page image. Leaves obscuring everything but her bare hands. A lump of leaves, maybe some hair sticking out, maybe an eye. But the hands are what draw the attention, the nails bent and broken, scratches and blood. Grim. The headline says another missing teen found. She was still alive. This was the last of the missing

I guess she's in the Sleep Room now, too. Books. Stack of books. I want to crawl into them. I want to stop existing. I glance at the newspaper. The last of the missing: found. Was it the work of Clara's mom and her cult? Rowan and his little group of poets?

Should I try and stop this? How many more are going to go missing in my city, my home where I see so many of my classmates wind up in the pines? I can't read. I try to read. I can't read.

I feel something waking up inside of me.

But the water pushes it down and away from me.

Fuck it. I close the book.

The hospital is only a block and a half away from the library. I need to see if my dad has gotten in to see my brother. I needed to see the Sleep Room. I needed to talk to nurses, to sneak peeks at health charts, to see how he was doing somehow. Someone had to give me information.

I can't keep going on like this. This wasn't being alive. This was just barely living.

On the way over, my phone buzzes: a text from Stacey.

Are you okay?

I pause. I thought I'd answered this before, but maybe she's worried about me?

I respond. *No.*

Neither am I. My friends here? They're missing. I know you're going through this too. Something is happening. Something is changing. I'm not okay. Nothing is okay. Not anymore, not now.

And I don't hear from her again until later that night.

Of course, I can't get into the Sleep Room, but the good part is neither could my dad. I saw him defeated in the waiting room outside. I sneaked a glimpse through the doors and saw these rows and rows of bodies, propped upright. Sleeping faces. I saw each of them were mutilated in different ways. Some with their eyes sewn shut like my brother, but some with them sewn wide open, and others with eyes missing. Some were missing hands, others had flowers shoved into wounds in their chest, the doctors unable to remove them without killing them outright. The roots had taken hold around their hearts, at least that's what I overheard from the orderlies. It made me sick to my stomach.

I didn't even say hello to my dad and he didn't seem to see me. Not right away. He was staring at his hands, ignoring everything around him. I couldn't tell if he was angry or sad or some liminal emotion that exists between the two. An emotion we don't have words for because you can't use words to express it. It's beyond words. It's something constructed out of colors and nothing else.

I walk past him like a ghost and I try and get information from everyone but him. But all of the nurses have apparently had their lips sewn shut, so that they couldn't speak to anyone about anything. I couldn't even glance at chart.

I should maybe ask my dad if he found anything out. But I don't want to speak to him. Not even about my brother. He's an intruder. He showed up too late. And now he pretends to act sad, act like he cared and put on the good dad mask.

Looking at him? I didn't feel anything. Just more emptiness. More of a void.

The rest of my afternoon is spent in the graveyard, sitting on Clara's tombstone, drinking a jug of cheap-ass wine I shoplifted from the Circle K near the hospital. I don't feel any less numb or lonely while doing it, but somehow it's comforting.

Not like it will bring her back. Not like I could save her.

It doesn't seem right that she died. I tried to save her and she still died.

Fuck this. Fuck her mom. Fuck *this*.

Eventually, I wander with tipsy legs and stutter and cling onto trees and gates. I make my way back to the outside. Walking through the gates felt electric. Like walking from one world to another. The sun is setting and the sky is red.

And I really… Fuck.

I really.

Fuck.

I miss her.

During the walk, I sober up. I think of going to the abandoned school where we used to go but it's too soon for that. It would be too much. The memories would be suffocating. I don't want that. I don't want to be suffocated by her ghosts.

I want to give up. It's too much. All of it too much. I am so drained. I'm not sure if I can feel anything anymore. Since Clara's death, all my emotions have drained out of my body.

Even if I could...even if I could stop them here in my city, it wouldn't end. It's spreading. It's now affecting Stacey, too. I didn't look it up online, but I know if I did, there would be panic everywhere as this fear spreads. How can I stop it? It's viral. It's destructive. It's all around me and I can't do anything.

Are you near a wall?

I look over. I'm inside the library again. Mostly because no place else will let me wander in without money. They're going to close in an hour, but I'm here again.

The wall I'm near is stone. The kind of stone that made this a bomb shelter during the Cold War. You can still see the signs all over. Signs that don't mean anything anymore. No more bombs in the air. No more threat of destruction hanging over our heads.

Yes. I text back.

It doesn't take long for Stacey to respond.

Good. Can you get some white chalk?

What? That seems like such an odd request. I look through my things. No chalk. I didn't expect to find any, anyway.

I don't know. Why?

As I wait for Stacey to respond I think more about the chalk. I think they have a blackboard in one of the learning rooms where they hold computer classes for people, oddly enough. Maybe there?

I don't know.

I need you to draw a chalk door on that wall.

I glance around. Nobody sees me.

I sneak into the learning annex. It's empty now and the lights are off. Old computers with giant monitors line the seats. Behind the teaching desk is an old blackboard, still covered in chalk, which looks multi-colored. White would be too simple, I guess.

Does it have to be white?

This whole room looks like it's from another time. It makes me wonder why that is? Maybe funding or some shit. I don't know. I walk over to the board and check the chalk tray. Broken pieces of chalk. Random blackboard erasers. I don't see white.

Yes. It has to be white.

I notice the desk drawers. Maybe in one of these? I need to hurry. I don't want to get caught. I slide them open and find brand new chalk in an unopened box: white. I put it in my pocket. Drawing a door in here is too risky.

The door to the annex swings open a little more.

"Hello? Hello?"

My least favorite librarian, Miss Bates stands there, blocking the entrance and tapping her foot. Her arms are crossed and her gaze over her glasses is one of spite and anger. She never seemed to like me before, but this kind of reaction was just unsettling.

"You aren't supposed to be in here. What are you doing in here?"

I stutter. "I, ugh, dunno. Got lost?"

She turns off the light. "Get out. Now. This isn't some place for you to smoke weed or whatever, so forget about it."

"Okay." I walk towards the exit.

She looks over me, and I noticed her expression change in a heartbeat. It softens for a moment, and there is a sadness there I never would've expected. It touches me, and I feel embarrassed for some reason. Anger was something I could deal with, something I expected from her. But this? This mix of pity and sadness? I wasn't sure I could take this.

"I know. I'm sorry about all that stuff that happened. But I can't let you in here, okay Hazel?"

I feel like I'm blushing. Everything is raw and open and I'm exposed, all skinless. I slide past her, hiding my face. I can't let her see my emotions.

Whatever Stacey is planning better be worth it. A voice over the intercom says that the library is closing in five minutes. I grab my bag. Walk out single file with the rest. I can make the chalk door on the outside of the library. I'm sure it won't matter.

I crawl along the outside wall of the library until I'm behind the building. I'm by the lake where the boats are floating and the sun is broken. I feel like stained glass, easily shattered by rocks.

I'm away from all eyes.

Okay. I text.

Okay. Stacey responds.

I draw the door. This is stupid, I think. This can't be right. I look over at it. It looks like the outline they draw around dead bodies in crime scenes. I think maybe that's it. Maybe I'm marking where a door was murdered. Professor Purple did it in the library with the butter knife.

A hand comes through the stone. Fingers grasping the air.

My breath is caught in a trap in my lungs. A lung-trap for my words. For breaths..

Then, an arm.

I can't remember how to breathe? Why can't I remember how to breathe? It's like something is hugging me tight, squeezing my lungs shut.

Then, a head. Stacey. I barely recognize her. It's been so long.

I feel like I'm going to faint.

Her legs step through, then her torso, skirt dancing around her hips. She falls forward, gasping. Hands on dirt. Knees on grass.

My breath returns to me. Inhale, exhale. What the fuck happened? I'm on the ground, crawling on all fours, the world spinning and everything becomes a pinpoint of light, and I'm close to blacking out, I can feel it, the fuzzy edges of reality closing on me. I bite my cheek; the pain makes me present again. I almost fainted. What the fuck happened?

"Hi!" Stacey gasps, trying to regain her ability to speak again.

I lean over and hug her and I try not to cry. It's been so long. It's been too long. Seeing her again is like being home. I never had a home, but the Safe House was as close to a home as I could get to it. I'm not crying. I wish I could because that would express the mixture of elation and sorrow I feel, but I'm not crying. The waves recede. Seeing her again makes me miss them all.

And there, there, right in my ribs. I feel it.

A spark. A little glimpse of fire. Of light.

We're done hugging but we can't move just yet. Motion seems like something that would end all of this and we don't want it to end. Not ever. Like moving forward would be leaving things behind. So, we sit. We watch the boats. Their sails are like rainbows in the water, moving about in slow motion. There, under the setting sun. There.

"Why did you..." I start to ask.

"I can't do it on my own."

"Do what?"

Stacey ignores my question. "We have to stop all of this. All the murders. You know that, right?"

"But how...how can we? It's spreading, isn't it? Like a virus, it's moving from person to person. All of these poems like diseases...how can we stop an idea?"

Stacey looks down at her hands. Her fingers are intertwined.

"Maybe this idea...maybe it grows when it infects people. It's not like a virus jumping, breeding and spreading. But maybe it's like, like this *thing* that grows. A single organism that spreads out, and it gets bigger and bigger."

"What the hell? Still. How do we stop it?"

Stacey has serious eyes. "We find the nucleus. And I think it's here."

"Here?"

"Where it started."

My heart thumps loudly in my chest, a wild animal trying to escape. I don't want this to be true, but I know it to be true. "Here."

"Yup. Come on." Stacey stands up, backpack slung over her shoulder. "First, let's get some chow. Man! Traveling through the holes in the universe sure takes a lot out of a girl. I'm starved! Let's go! Let's go!"

I move forward to lead the way, and she grabs my arm. "Wait," she says, "Wherever we go needs to have free Wi-Fi."

"Why?"

"So I can show you something."

I nod. "There is a coffee house that does. It doesn't have the best eats, but it's something."

She shoves me forward. "What are we waiting for? Heeya! Mush! Mush!"

That spark inside spreads just a little. A quiet little flame and the smallest breath could blow it out forever. But there it is like candles, dipping one to the other, lighting their little flames, whispering in the cathedral of my ribs.

The coffee house is near the lake so it's not too far from the library. It's a round place with windows encircling it, giving all the people inside a panoramic view of the hill and the lake and everything. It's almost as if we're floating. Like we're having coffee on a raft moving out to sea without all that rocking and seasick feeling.

I'm having a simple coffee and Stacey has a pile of multi-colored donuts in front of her, displayed in a rainbow of chocolate, crispy glazes, and strawberry filling. She greedily starts picking up donut after donut, devouring them, the crumbs tumbling down her face. She's busy swiping at her tablet and typing on a virtual keyboard, not even paying attention.

I'm looking around us, paranoid. What if one of the Susans were here? What would I do? How would I react? I don't see them though. Not Rowan and his crew, not the Susans, not even Clara's mom.

Stacey taps my arm. "Okay, this website here? You can't google it. You can only get to it if you know the exact IP address. It's not like, completely hidden? You don't need a password to get in. Just finding it's the hard part. Someone doesn't want people to find it. Or maybe, they want people to feel like they accomplished something finding it."

"How did you find it?"

She looks at the ceiling, covers her mouth with her hand, as if stifling back some overwhelming emotion, as tears dot the edges of her eyes. Then she slides the tablet towards me. "My sis went missing. And um...they never found her. I mean, some people claim they see her...in the trees. In their closets at night. Anyway. Yeah. She just... was gone. One day just gone." Stacey pauses. "And so, I decided to investigate, I found her diary. Crazy shit in there. Crazy, crazy shit about poems. About some poet that was around in the 1930's or something. Anyway, in there? There was this IP address. I typed it in, and look what I found."

I glance down at the tablet. The fire stirs. Something in my bones wakes up again.

I don't want to look at the tablet but it tugs on me, dragging me towards it. The website wants to infect me; I can feel it. The page is old looking, like an ancient Internet-era homepage. Plain text black background. Pictures all over. It's about some poet who collaborated with Surrealists. And then, he came to the US, he was a key part of so much death here. It shows graphic pictures. It shows bodies arranged. It has his poems. It has his face.

It doesn't have his name.

I don't want to read his poems. Not the word poems; not the physical poems carved into people. The poems of murder, the poems without. There is even a forum but I didn't click on it. I didn't want to see it.

I hand the tablet back to Stacey. I want to throw up whatever is trying to infect me, whatever is worming around inside of me. I feel it going after the fire and I recoil just a little, pushing back, not wanting it to touch the flames. These are my flames. I lick them out, the edges singing whatever it is inside of me, serpent-strong, and I just keep my head down. I make the fire bigger inside and it burns like a forest burns. Bigger and bigger. The tentacles of flame inside of me, fighting the infection like white blood cells. Everything spins dizzy but I stay calm, I stay grounded, not going to get sick, not going to throw up. No, no, not me.

My hands shaking, I finally look up. I see a reflection of fear in her eyes, proud and defiant. She knew this would happen, she knew, I could see it in that gaze.

"You could've warned me."

Stacey shakes her head. "No, you need to see what I'm talking about. Do you see it now?"

I shiver now head to toe, and I want to scream. The infection moving, wrapping around my bones. The flames lick out some more, push it back, and I am feverish with poetry. "Fuck. Fuck. Fuck."

"Drink some of this." She pulls a thermos out of her bag. "Just some tea. It helps. Well, it helped me, at least."

I unscrew the cap and sniff it. Foul. Fucking foul. "What is it?"

"Tea," Stacey asserts

"It doesn't smell like any fucking tea I've had. Like, ever."

"It's made from...flowers I found."

"Yeah?"

"Flowers growing on graves. Fuck. Just drink it. It will help."

I pinch my nose and drink it and drink some more and--

That is bad. Oh, damn it, it tastes so fucking bad. I almost spit it out but I force it down my throat down into my stomach. It burns and my fire flickers a little brighter. After a moment, that worm inside is gone.

"Okay. You feel better now?"

"Yeah. I guess I do. What's the plan going forward?"

"We need to find the entry point, and maybe get to the center and just stop it."

"Entry point?"

"Yeah, you know. Like where did it start? The origin of it all."

"Oh."

"Any ideas?"

And I have no ideas. Not about an "entry point." But I think of Clara's mom. And I say, "But I might now who is at the head of all this."

"Good. Let's go kill the head and watch the body rot."

Does it get any easier? I don't know…I just…fuck. I can't stop thinking about Clara, or Dylan, or any of those heads in a circle. But Clara's the hardest. Every moment of every day I feel lost. Like any second, she's going to call me. Or stop by. Or pick me up. Or tell me to meet her somewhere. Or bitch about her mom. And this makes me laugh and sob and choke on my thoughts. Her mom. I guess she had every right to bitch about her.

I feel like I'm falling into darkness and the light is dim and floating above me. I feel those waves come again to numb me. The only thing that keeps that spark dancing and alive is the fact that I can stop it. I keep these thoughts to myself and sink further under shadows, the light above me going smaller and smaller and smaller. I want to reach up. I don't want to reach up. I want to sink and sink and sink and sink…

I sigh with my whole body and say, "It's been a long time, um, since the Safe House and stuff."

Stacey leans back against the wall. "I know."

"Do you miss it?"

"I miss it sometimes, yes." And her eyes close and I can tell she's trying hard not to cry. It hurts to talk about it, I know. It hurts me too.

"I miss having other people around who understood. Like, deep down understood that need to just destroy yourself. Most people think of it as suicide or something, but that's not it. It's, like, the pain of existing is so great that destroying yourself is the only thing that makes sense. It's the only thing you can control, the only thing that makes you feel real anymore."

Stacey puts her arm around me and we just sit like that. She rubs her arm over my back and we're silent for a few moments.

"Does it ever get any easier?"

Stacey mutters in a sad, low voice. "No. Not for people like us. We'll always be haunted by the scars of our past."

When I look in the mirror in the bathroom, I see Clara's face and something moving in the shadows of the stalls. The doors are open. I want to shut them all. I wash my face. The water is cool..

Maybe screaming will make her go away. I want to scream.

But

But

But

I don't want her to go away. Oh fuck, I miss Clara so much. I close my eyes and I can almost feel her near me. Maybe a hand on my shoulder. Maybe her breath in my hair whispering some secret. I've known her for almost my whole life and now that she's gone, there is a hole in everything. I can see the holes everywhere. That the physical nature of everything is just a prop. A drape hung over empty holes. Trying to disguise the void in everything.

Clara is now part of that void.

I open my eyes and she's gone. There is nothing but flickering neon. And this feeling like my whole skin is on fire. Prickles cover me all over. I want to walk through this and let it all go through me. Where are my knives when I need them?

The spark is shaking. The spark is spreading. I feel the fire again. I feel the scream again. I want to explode and take everything with me. I kick a stall door and I remember Dylan hung over a similar stall. It's almost like I'm kicking his corpse.

I see smoke; I see fire, see sparks where my shoe hit the wood. There's the fire. There it is. The fire sings, sings the songs of my childhood. It sings the songs I used to sing with Clara as we rode the bus on countless field trips.

The fire is spreading across the bathroom, and I'm laughing because this doesn't scare me anymore. Nothing scares me anymore. The fire will not consume me, but it will consume everything else.

I walk out of the bathroom, smoke all around me.

"Come on," I say to Stacey, "Let's go."

Stacey looks back at the bathroom. Nobody else is looking there. No one in the whole place. They're all staring at other things: each other, computers, tablets, their phones, e-readers. The fire does not register. The smoke does not register. But Stacey sees it and she smiles. Thin corners of her lips jerking back.

"Holy fucking shit. Hazel. Shit. Holy shit. Hazel. Who are you?"

I want to start a fight. I want to swallow this rage and spit it in their face. I am the hollow girl filled with light and knives. Kiss me. I am the sun. I will burn them up with one touch of these lips. Fireworks follow me like leaves in the fall. The words I cull from my brain are the words of electrical fires.

We're walking away as ambulances speed past us. It's like I can feel the sirens in my bones. I feel them rumbling and the fire engines roaring. All these machines scrambling towards the coffee house.

Stacey walks next to me, holding her bag to her chest like a shield, her chin pressed against the straps.

I feel like everything around me is ready to catch fire and all I have to do is just touch it. Just a single touch and I can make it all go up in flames.

"So..." Stacey says.

"So."

"You said, uh, the head. Right?"

"Yeah. The head."

A pause as we walk. The fire reflects on the lake behind us.

"Are you? Are you the..."

"No."

I breathe. It feels so good to breathe. I feel something on my cheek. Something wet. Something like a tear? I don't even know what to call it. Am I crying? "No, I'm not."

I can't think of Clara right now or her mom. I know I need to, but I need to rest for a moment. My brain needs to breathe.

"Then...what was...what was that?"

I keep walking. I can't look behind. Looking behind? It's death.

"That was...that was me, mourning everything."

"Everything?"

I wipe my cheeks. My face is so wet. My hands touch my skin and I'm so hot. Fire inside giving me a fever and I laugh a little, just a few laughs and wipe my face with my arms.

"Yeah," I say, "Yeah everything. All this shit, Like all this shit and everything. I'm mourning my brother, and fuck, I'm mourning Clara and all those missing people... You know, I don't think I even knew them but I mourn them.

"And I'm mourning my life. My fucking life! It was messy and it was nasty but it was my fucking life! And now here: look at all this shit. Look at all of it. It's all broken and busted up. Look at all those dead friends I have, you know? Fuck. Even Dylan; that asshole.

"I mourn my life because now? Now I feel like my whole life is spent grieving. I grieve the life I was supposed to have, you know? All that suburban shit. The childhood that was taken from me when I was put in that fucking Safe House. I mourn all of it. Fuck it. Fuck it."

I'm laughing and wiping more tears.

"I've got nothing left anymore but the shattered bones of all this and I can't put it back together without it all falling apart again. Fuck. I'm not even making sense anymore! None of it makes any sense anymore! And how can it? I'm made of fire. I'm filled with the fire that made the waves go away. And nothing…. Nothing is everywhere.

Holes in everything, everywhere."

Stacey listens to all of it. She just listens patiently. And then she says, "Well, it makes sense to me. Not in the logistics way, you know? But in a gut way. I get that emotional crash that your feeling, Kind of. I don't get all of it, but I get some of it. Okay?"

I nod and my head feels like a jack in the box.

"Okay."

"Now we're lucky, right? We're lucky right now. Do you know why?"

"Why?"

"Because we can make it all right. We can't bring back the dead, but we can sure as fuck avenge them. Can't we? We can. So, let's do it. Let's go and make things a little less wrong, let's make all this shit a little more right. Let's grab that head and smash it in. Then we can find the entry point together, right? And we can close it all off."

"All right."

We walk a little further, up the hill and towards the skyscrapers looking down over the lake. The fire and commotion are behind us. It's far enough away that it sounds like it's happening to someone else. And I say, "Although, there is one thing."

"Yeah?"

"You suck at these inspirational speeches."

And we both smile. It feels good to smile.

"Yeah, I know. But you feel better, right?"

"Just a little. Come on, let's do this shit."

My dress is rags soaked in gasoline.
My heart is a spark.
Watch me burn with the light of ghosts.

The house. Her house. So many memories. That house. We are in the garden. We climbed over the fence by the pines.

I remember the last time I did that. Fuck. Me and Clara running. The knives out. The slumber party gone wrong. Clara dying. Me trying to stop it.

Clara dying.

Me not being able to stop it.

Come on.

Suck it the fuck up.

Come on.

I need to let these feelings burn me up and push me forward. I can't let them suck me down and drown me. The light from the living room shines through the glass doors. I can see the kitchen. Everything feels so different. The void is in all of it. I see holes inside of everything. I can feel the light of memories leaking from them.

I want to scream. The scream is inside of me. My bones are burning. I want to carve this world apart with the sounds of my screaming.

Stacey moves forward, crouching behind trees. Then bushes. We dart behind things, shadows hiding our bodies. I don't know what the plan is? I think Stacey has a plan. I hope Stacey has a plan. I don't have a plan. Maybe I don't need one. Maybe I just need to let all of this out and have the fire kill Clara's mom. Maybe that will make everything all right. I don't want Stacey to die. There are too many dead friends.

Stacey motions me to come up next to her. We're both hiding behind these bushes now and we can see inside. We can see bodies in the living room. The slumber party girls. They are all there, sitting in the middle of the living room. Clara's mom is in the middle. Candles are everywhere.

Another sacrifice. A new one.

The fire is roaring inside of me now. Anger and frustration like waves, and we have to stop it, we need to stop this. We will silence this poem before they can even get it started.

"What's the plan?" I ask Stacey.

"Shit. Well. I didn't know that there would be so many people here."

My head bows to the ground. "They killed Clara."

"Your friend? The one...before the Safe House. That one?"

I don't answer and she knows that she's right.

"Okay. I just didn't expect any of this."

We curl our bodies up against each other to try and keep ourselves hidden in the shadows. The moon is overhead and caught in the finger-bones of the trees.

All those ghosts in my skin are stirring, all the fire sparking up again. My mouth tastes like ashes; my fingers smell like coal. The thought of climbing that fence, of running through this garden. The sound Clara made as they stabbed her over and over again… It was like a sigh. Almost hopeful.

"Hazel? You okay?"

I growl because those are the words of the fire. Growling and sparking and crackling.

She slowly moves back. I feel drums in my heart, feel them pushing the flames, feel them all white and glowing. My hair floats over my head like fire in space.

Stacey scoots back, her eyes wide.

"This is it. Isn't it? This is it."

"They *killed* Clara."

She watches as I stand, as I walk forward. There is fire in the shape of my shoe prints in the dirt. I walk towards the glass doors to see my reflection.

But all I see? All I see is Clara engulfed in flames. Her body burning and her face? It's ecstasy. And I think—I hope—she has that now, that feeling she craved. The spiritual ecstasy she saw in pain.

I slide open the glass door.

Time stops.

I walk through the door to the kitchen and fire follows me. This is the kitchen where we played and pretended to cook with her mom's pots and pans. Where we woke up to her mom making us pancakes and bacon. This is where I came for solace after I got back from Safe House and my dad left us. This is where we would hang out and eat snacks later after high school and talk stupid shit. This is where Dylan first called me and asked me out, back before he became someone else.

I walk to the living room. Time is frozen as I move. Everything is like a slow-moving dream. I see the steps going upstairs to Clara's room and the door leading down to the basement. I remember all the times we crawled down to that basement, the cold stone walls like a dungeon. Where we hung lanterns and tried to contact the dead.

Now. Fuck. Now Clara's one of the dead. And it's like I'm always contacting her. She's always everywhere. There is no silence from her ghost. It moves me forward. It makes the light in my heart burn brighter. I am fire. This is her fire. I am her ghost. This is her ghost fire.

I'm in the doorway to the living room. Her mom is at the head of the circle, looking directly at me. They're all wearing blue dresses and they all stare at me in a mixture of hate and fear. Their bodies vibrating with violence, and their eyes wide in terror when they see me.

I spread my arms. I can still hear Clara playing guitar and singing and everything is just wrong now.

None of them say anything. No one speaks.

I look at them.

"This is our poetry," Clara's mom finally says. "We bring you here to show you what makes everything beautiful."

I speak with the voice of fire. "You didn't bring me here."

They don't argue.

The fire rises up, typhoons of terrifying power, and I feel the heat from the inside, my heart combusting in light and it doesn't hurt, instead it feels so overwhelmingly beautiful. Like the one time I went to the ledges by the lake. I stood on the edge, and looked down, down, down at the roaring waves far below, at least a mile of jutting rock with tiny outcrops of trees, and I thought it was so beautiful, so damned beautiful. I remember having tears in my eyes. And I felt no fear, no anger, just this overwhelming sense of oneness with everything. I thought if I jumped it would somehow complete the beauty. My death, without fear, without sorrow, would perfect this moment. And that is how I feel now, an echo of that moment right now, the beauty and terror of the fire overwhelming me as it rushes out of me. My whole body burning bright light, and I swear I hear the fire singing, singing with the voices of all the dead.

"Here is my poetry," I whisper, my limbs growing numb and distant. Here is the beauty I bring the world, as I collapse and the floor greets my face. Everything is a numb pinprick of light, and I had no idea how much the fire was keeping me going until this moment, this moment here. When it leaves, and my limbs become numb anchors, and my mind turns into this fuzzy, spinning dot.

And then darkness descends and I smile. I smile as I dip further away from the world, my fire no longer animating my body, my own poetry set free. I slide into dreaming.

I dream again of the Dead Snake Tree. I no longer fear what it means. Not anymore. I think I know what this is.

The start. The entry point.

It's this dream. This dream here. The Dead Snake Tree is the start, the end; it is a circle.

When I wake up, I am tied down. I can smell the strange coppery smell of the lake just before the storm, and I can hear the wish-wash sound of waves around me, and the soft cries of seagulls. I'm still in that after-dream disorientation, and I wonder if I actually jumped from the ledges above, and I'd forgotten it somehow.

How did I even get here? Didn't my fire burn the world? Wasn't that my revenge, my poetry, my salvation? Did I even stop that final sacrifice?

Am I the final sacrifice?

Everything moves around me again. Every object and every *thing* is full of kinetic energy. I'm exhausted just looking at it, any of it.

I try and move my arms and the ties are pretty thick and strong. Rope? Not metal, at least that much I know. Maybe plastic? I can't tell.

I hear the rush of water. I turn my head and I see the lake. I turn my head the other way and I see cliff faces towering over me. I don't know where Stacey is. I don't know what happened. I feel lost and my fire is gone.

Did I burn them all? Are they all dead now? Is Clara's spirit finally quiet?

I feel like choking. Sand is in my mouth. Sand is in my throat.

I sleep again for a while. My whole body aches. Everything feels raw. Open and bleeding. I cough. I can't stop coughing.

Eventually, I open my eyes again. The sun is low near the waves. I don't know what time it was, how long I've been out.

I hear footsteps coming my way.

My fire should've destroyed everything, and now it's all gone and I feel so lonely without it. I try to call out for help but my mouth is full of sand and my throat aches, and I try and wiggle out of my bounds but I can't do it. I search for the fire inside of me again, but it's gone. Empty. I am nothing without it.

I let the waves crash against my body as I spit out sand and let out a hoarse scream before my mouth fills with water.

The footsteps kick closer. Lots and lots and lots of footsteps. And voices. Little girl voices and little girl laughter.

I turn over and see their shiny black shoes. The water rushes up over them and then rushes back. All black shoes all alike. Little girl legs attached to them. All those little girls wearing bird masks again. All of the beautiful little masks. Colors like rainbows, each of the masks different birds. A robin, a starling, a bluebird, and on and on. "Roll over," one whispers from behind the plastic.

I'm so numb now. I roll over. I feel sharp cutting and the binds break away. My wrists and my hands are free. I push myself up, knees clutched to chest. The sun stares at me. I feel empty, like everything flowed out of me and left me hollow and broken and I don't want to be alive.

"You aren't responsible for any of it," the one says.

I don't know what to say. "Any of it?"

Another little girl says, "Your brother is awake. You should go to him."

All of the birds nod. I try and stand up. My legs wobble wobble wobble. They help me regain my balance. "Thanks," I say and then try walking forward a little at a time. I have no idea how long I've been there. "How did you guys find me?"

One looks at me and her eyes are so serious. None of these girls joke. That I can tell. Even with masks on their faces, that I can tell.

"None of this is real. It's easy to see that none of this is real. We're all waiting for everything to end, aren't we? How can we be real if we're constantly waiting for the world to end? If it's real, then everything matters. If the world ends? Then nothing matters. So, none of this is real."

She spoke my fears out loud. They weren't my fears anymore. They are like the fears of strangers. Of a different person. Where these the fears of the dead? Where they the fears of corpses or the memories of those that passed on?

"Am I ghost?"

"No. We are stars lost in the ocean," one says.

"We are lightning trapped in the mouths of giants," says another.

"No one here is a ghost. Not today, anyway," says yet another.

They help me walk. This murder of little girls surrounds me, helping me move up over the beach to the street. They help me sit down in a bus shelter and we wait. We wait as the rain starts to come down around us. We wait for the bus. We are not ghosts. But I feel like a ghost, like a whisper from the past caught in the present.

This rain is not real rain. This bus is not a real bus. I look behind me at the bus shelter as the not-real bus lurches forward. The bird girls are gone. Only stacks of masks remain, waiting for someone to pull them on. To make themselves into something else.

Was reality a mask? Could I take it off and see the holes everywhere? The void everywhere? Like the Dead Snake Tree in my dream. Could I shrink myself down into something tiny and crawl into the holes of reality? Maybe. Maybe? Maybe.

The bus moves into traffic. Everything is slow going, even the rain. The rain in the sunshine. I sit and look out the window as we wind our way through the world. I keep hoping somehow I would see Clara. Like, her boarding the bus or maybe her walking down some random street. Or maybe sitting outside of a coffee house, squatting on concrete and drinking from a brown cup.

But she's not there. She's not anywhere. She's gone. Fog appears in the daylight, too. The bus stops and a whole group of foxes run across the street. If I look one way? They are foxes. If I look the other way? People. The missing ones, the ones who disappeared. The ones that became heads and limbs and all of that. The ones who were in comas in the Sleep Room with my brother. They run across the street in the rain.

The halls of the hospital are tight with family members, some getting happy reunions right away. Others needing help. But all of the people in the Sleep Room? All of them are awake now. Every single last one.

I look for my mom, or my dad, or my brother, or any of them. Eventually, I fight my way to the front, and try to catch the attention of the nurse behind the desk. She isn't paying attention to me, trying hard to do something on the computer monitor in front of her. A line of people fidget behind me, angry. I don't care, I'm not going anywhere, not until she helps me out. I rap on the desk and clear my throat

"Yes?" She's irritated. I can tell. Good.

"I'm sorry, I need your help. My brother? Is he still here? He was..."

"Yeah," she says, her voice like heavy smoke. "He was the first to wake up. Quite a star, your brother, you know? Lots of people sniffing around asking questions. Cops, reporters, bloggers, all that shit. You should be prepared when you go up and see him."

"Prepared?"

"Yeah. Quite a crowd around him. Quite a crowd."

I nod and she gives me his room number and I walk towards the elevator. I remember Dylan trying to push his way through to see me, to embrace me. I shiver. But I remember, no, he's dead. I saw the body. I set his head on fire. Still, I think about it and I against my better judgment, I picture his mutilated ghost running towards me, head a basket of flames, trying to force his way in yet again.

The elevator doors close and I'm alone. The tune over the speakers sounds like sad music boxes. I slump against the wall and I put my head in my hands and wish for the world to end again. I want it all to end. The fire inside of me is gone and I miss it. I miss the drive and determination that ran around inside of me like an earthquake. Yes, it was painful. Yes, it made me want to destroy myself.

But now my mind is a beach with these waves of numb shadows crashing against it. That's all. Numb waves and the lake calling out to me. I picture in my head blue: blue and the lake rising up, getting larger and larger on the hills. Then crash! The water goes down and everything in the city sinks lower and lower until there is nothing left. We're all floating in the waves, back flat and sleeping, like all these bodies stacked underwater.

I am so numb. The elevator goes up.

There he is. Sitting upright with a tray on his lap. Machines still plugging in under his skin. His head's shaved. He has electrodes resting against his skull. He's eating oatmeal and he's smiling. Mom and Dad are next to him, and a gold beam of light comes in from the window. Outside, I hear birds and they sing to each other.

I feel like I'm being ripped to shreds.

He looks at me. "Oh my god! Hazel!"

"Casper, oh, Casper..." I'm crying a little. Fuck.

"Oh shit, Hi sis," he says, and then sets the oatmeal down and swings the tray aside.

I nod and then say, "Can I hug you? I mean. All those wires. Can I hug you?"

He motions me with his hands and I run over and we embrace for a while. We sit there like that and I hear Mom and Dad leave the room. I need this. We both need this.

I pull back. "I thought I lost you."

He puts his hand on my face. "You did, Hazel. I was lost and wandering around. But it was for a long time, way before the coma, way before all of it. I was lost and looking for something. And then I thought...well, I thought something found me."

"I know, sort of."

"You know how you feel a long dream, and it takes a minute but then you see you're not dreaming anymore? And everything is just clear? There is such a clarity. It's so bright and blinding."

"Clara's dead."

We pause for a moment.

"And Dylan, he's dead too. And others. Oh, Casper. What did you get yourself mixed up in?"

He looks down at his bed. "I thought it was over but I can feel it still. Can't you feel it, Clara? There is something wrong with the world."

"I thought it was...clear now?"

He still isn't looking at me. He's glancing everywhere but at my face. This unnerves me, he can't be right. It has to be over, after all we went through, after everything I've gone through?

He rubs his eyes for a bit, and I can still the marks from where they'd sewn it shut. "It's clear. Yes. It is clear. And that's what I mean? They think it's poetry, but it's not. It's ritual. He knew it, when he saw it. He called it poetry, but he was looking for a rebirth."

And my brother stops rubbing his eyes, and places his hands on his lap. His eyes are bloodshot red, and I feel this sense of dread. I know he's right, in my gut, in my bones. I know it even though I don't want to be right. I feel reality turning into a pinprick of light once again, as he continues.

"Now? Now. Now it's everywhere, in everything. The infection is spreading, and the ritual commences, and now everything is wrong. Can't you see how wrong everything is? The light is sucked out and it's all desaturated. Like the colors are slowly losing their life and becoming ghosts of what they were." And I have noticed that, and I thought it was because of the fire leaving me, of all the ghosts leaving me. But no, it's more than that. My brother sees it, too.

"Everything is a ghost now! We're all haunted by a reality that no longer exists. We live in shadows. Can't you see it Hazel? We live in shadows."

Everything spins and my numbness is stronger now, an anchor in my heart. Of course it's not over, of course it will never be over. That's the way the world is, isn't it? A cycle of suffering repeating itself over and over again.

I know what Casper will say next before he even says it.

"Others will die."

And then he pulls his tray back and starts eating his oatmeal again in silence.

I try to talk to Mom and Dad but they're silent about everything, like they're glad he's back and glad he's not. Dad's talking about leaving again tonight, now that his little boy's okay. I wonder if this was all just a big show for him. Like, he liked pretending to be compassionate at moments of crisis and if that's not the case, if he can't wear the hero mask and prance around all big and strong, then he doesn't need to be around.

Mom's silent though and I try to talk and nothing comes out. I wonder if Casper coming back constructed a wall around us. The things he's been through...How can any of us understand?

He needs a walker now. For everything. He can feed himself, but barely. He can talk, but his words slur and sometimes he gets them all mixed up. Not often, but often enough. How will life be like for us, for him?

I hate to admit it, but now I'm uncomfortable around my brother. It's like being around someone else. Maybe like talking to a photograph of my brother. One that is crumpled up and burned.

Shit. Fuck. I'm a terrible person. I know I am. I am a terrible person.

I leave the hospital. I can't stand being there anymore. I get a call from Stacey's phone but it's all static and maybe crackling like fire crackles and sighs from boiling water. Shit, I wonder if my phone got damaged the other day at the lake. It's not cracked, but the sand and water maybe messed it up. I text her, asking if she's okay. I still don't know what happened the other night. But the waves inside of me don't care. All I feel is emptiness. Even towards my brother. Towards everyone. Just emptiness.

I know the truth now. I see the truth everywhere now. Emptiness, emptiness, emptiness. The physical world is just a mask for the emptiness all around us. The numb waves inside wrap around my heart, and I know I miss the flame so much. The fire was my own poetry; I know that now. I wonder if I could get it back, somehow. If I became a poem myself, if the fire would come back to me, ghosts and all. Would it save me from this horrible empty world?

I could just call Rowan up, give myself over to him. Let him turn me into a poem and watch the fire come back to me. I hear the numb waves whispering this to me, telling me the secret of it all. To become a poem, according to the waves, is the only meaning to this horrible empty existence. To become art is to achieve permanence, to actually be something. Instead of a hollow, empty, nothing, filled with the sound of the ocean.

Is this how the others felt? Did the waves call to them, talk them into becoming poetry? Maybe so. It just feels so right.

To become a poem. Just so right.

I turn on my phone. I search through my contacts. I call Rowan's number.

"Hey, Hazel." He sounds sleepy, irritated, and yet somehow hopeful. Like he knew I was going to call. Like he knew that I would need him to make me into a poem.

"I'm ready. Come find me." I hang up.

I lay down on the sidewalk. People walk around me. Some over me. I see car wheels on the street. Close to the curb, close to my face. And I smile. It's a numb smile and it feels right. All of this feels right. The hot light against the waves under my skin. The poetry singing to me. It all feels so right.

Can you teach me how to breathe?

All reality is just objects floating in space. Everything is emptiness. Between us is all emptiness, all void. Can we breach this emptiness. If we can breach the gravity we create for ourselves... Do we have enough breath to float through space without suffocating...

Someone pulls me up by my shirt. I move like water moves, without any resistance, my limbs like waves as I flow upwards. Strong hands spin me around and I see Rowan standing there. He is without his group of poets.

My lips are numb and my words are dumb flailing things. They want to just leak out of my mouth and stumble down my lips on the ground.

Rowan's rocking back and forth, chewing on his fingernails, his eyes wide and panicked. His voice is shaking, gone is that smooth confidence of before. "Hazel? It's all different and it's all wrong. I don't know what's going on anymore. Hazel?" Hazel? Can you help me, Hazel? I'm terrified. I keep seeing images of this strange guy, with wild hair, and a girl that's trapped in a crystal. He's calling me to him, she's calling me…and it's so terrifying."

I start laughing. I can't stop. I want to stop and I can't. I'm almost falling over on the ground. And I don't even know what's so funny anymore. He is. Everything is. Nothing makes sense anymore. All I hear are the sounds of waves. They are all around me.

"Stop laughing! Snap out of it!" He turns, looks over his shoulder, hands flapping in the air like he was trying to shoo something away. "I told you this would be all fucked up. I didn't even know what she wanted when she called me. Why did you make me come down here?"

I look behind him and there is this little blind girl. She looks like Alice from Wonderland but her eyes are just white. She's even dressed in a blue pinafore and everything.

The sounds of waves stop when I see her. Everything stops. I feel so empty inside. Why do I feel so empty inside? I am drained of everything and, with the numb water gone, all I feel is pain. I am so full of pain. Everything inside of me hurts.

"You know my sisters," she says to me matter-of-factly. I recognize that intonation, that way of speaking…

"Yes," I say. My mouth isn't numb. But my words… They are painful to speak. All words hurt me. "I think. Yes. Bird masks, right?"

"Correct." A smile with her pretty teeth. Her tombstone teeth. All smile, those teeth.

"Why do I feel different when I'm around you?" I ask her.

"My sisters poured the waves of the night into your mouth and ears to help you through the transition. Your fire was stolen from you, and we know how lonely that can be. We wanted to numb you to that suffering. Rowan here? He doesn't know anything anymore. The urge to be a poet is gone, the spirit has left him. His friends are all dead now."

"They are?"

She reaches out a hand and touches me and her hands are so cold. "The Susans have stolen your fire. Now that the Poet has your fire, he is spreading faster and faster like a forest engulfed. That spark that was inside of you is burning the world down."

"Oh." I gulp and shirk away from her touch, like it was covered in a million insects. All of a sudden, I feel fizzy, like I'm filled with bubbles. Effervescent. Her mere touch sent my mind spinning.

"Rowan will show you the way to the Dead Snake Tree. You know what to do."

I'm having trouble standing up. I lean against Rowan, my head wobbling from side to side, as I vomit water across the floor. It tastes like fish and I feel even emptier than before. I am *so* empty. The only thing left is pain: the pain of emptiness.

"I'll do what?" Rowan says, looking at the little girl. "What will I do?"

The girl steps back. "You will show her Sleeping Beauty. You remember. You *remember*. It was the last thing you saw before the blackout, before waking up in the pines with a face in your hands."

He looks white and ghostly. "I don't want to remember that."

She doesn't say anything. She leaps into traffic and disappears among the moving cars, spinning between them in a ballet of flesh and metal.

I don't know if I can be okay. I don't know if I'll ever be okay. So empty. So painful. I ache with every movement. I want my heart to stop beating. I want this all to end.

Yet. *Yet*.

I move on.

Rowan's driving me back to the pines. Of course, the pines. Everything stops and starts there. The pain inside of me flares up. Like when you touch a burn.

Clara.

Oh, fuck. Where we found the heads and the butterflies.

Clara.

Rowan looks at me. He looks lost, like he's searching for something and I'm the only one that could help him find whatever it was.

"I think, maybe, we should turn around."

He panics. "No! No, oh god no. You can't, you can't do this to me. She promised me! She told me you could help me remember. You could make everything in my head fit together like some puzzle. I'm missing pieces you know? All these moments that are like dancing shadows on some cave wall. Fuck. You have to help me."

"Are you sure you want help?"

His lips quivering, his eyes darting about, manic, as his face jerked from side to side in a strange, almost mechanical way of moving. It's like something broke inside of him, the gears of his mind slipping away. "I woke up with my mom's face in my hands. Just her face. Fucking hell. I woke up in these pines and I saw that. And I don't want to go back there, okay? I don't want to do it. But we need to, okay? If we can make all of this right; we need to make this right somehow. I have a feeling I did some very bad shit and we need to fix it all, make the world right again. She said you could do that!" His face turns red as he screams. "She said you could do that!"

We're both quiet for a moment as he drives, his outburst hanging in the air between us. I'm shocked, every part of me tense with the promise of danger in his voice.

I think he senses the way I recoil from him slightly, and he loosens a little, his head rolling between his shoulders. I just wish he would keep his eye on the road now.

I understood the outburst in one way. I've felt that way, too. Lots of times since this whole crazy mess started. Still doesn't mean I'm comfortable with it, though. Or comfortable around Rowan at all.

"I'm sorry," Rowan says. "I'm so sorry. I didn't mean...I mean. We need to fix this."

"All right." My words feel like the words spoken by a stranger. "But I don't know if I can."

"Shit. Shit. Shit. Shit." He hammers on the wheel with the palm of his hands. "Shit. Well, fuck it. We're going there anyway."

We pull in and I see the gates and I know I'm right. We're back here, back to the old midway. It looks different in the sunlight, somehow, even more haunted. But beautiful? If that makes sense. Like all of my ghosts are now beautiful ghosts. I try not to think about Clara. I don't want to think about those heads.

"Okay." I unbuckle my seatbelt. "Show me this Sleeping Beauty."

Rowan pushes the car door open and fidgets. "I think...I think I know. It's all so fuzzy. When I remember things? I feel like I'm watching a mirror Rowan walking about. And he's um, how do I say this? Like he's moving like a puppet, and I can't control him. This is all fuzzy like a soft lens on a camera, you know?"

He seems so different now. Before, he had this charismatic pull like some cult leader. Now he a nervous wreck, and any moment he is going to fall apart and collapse right in front of me. "I can't remember much else before that. Like it was all a dream and now that I'm awake, it floats away. If I lose this, if I can't remember who I was back then, then I lose some horrible thing that happened to me. Maybe I want to lose it? If I can't be that person anymore, wouldn't that be a good thing? Maybe we don't need to be ourselves to be ourselves, if you know what I mean."

I resist rolling my eyes at his monologue; we're wasting time. We have things we need to do, and here he is trying to be all philosophical. "No, I don't. Come on, just show me the way."

He looks like he's going to scream and cry at the same time.

I get out of the car. The tall grass feels sharp against my skin. Everything is so sharp and painful. But I push through it. I have to keep pushing through this.

I want to be numb again or on fire again or anything again. This empty pain is worse.

I don't want to die or burn the world down or be made into poetry. But I just want to stop the pain, but I can't stop it.

I want to fill myself with anything. Drink fire, eat broken glass, whatever. The empty pain is more than I can take.

I just *can't* do this.

When I was cutting myself, there was a release and in that release came moments of peace. This pain... There is no release. I am the void now and the void hurts so much. This ache is in my veins and my heart and my bones. It is an epidermal pain, a muscle ache and broken ache. That's it, that's what I am. I am so broken.

Clara...

No. I can't think of that.

Clara...

`Rowan leads me` into the center of the midway. Trees grow up and burst through roller coaster tracks like woodsy hands spreading fingers. And then we move over to the lake and I see the old boats. We used to ride these across to the island in the center.

My bones ache and I feel like I need to sit but I know sitting won't help. Sitting will be painful, too. The air is painful. The sky is painful. I am the pain. That is what the world needs sometimes though. Sometimes the world needs pain.

"Do you know how to drive one of those things?"

Rowan shakes his head. "No, we're going to take the life raft. That's what mirror Rowan did last time, and I think we should probably do it again and not risk fate."

`Small little raft of a thing.` We ride it across the water towards the small island in the center of the lake. I remember doing this before. I remember what they used to have on that island. All of those bars, all of those robot pirates pretending to swash-buckle and shoot muskets at each other. I wonder if robots can have ghosts.

I look down at the water as we paddle. I put my hand in. I see green things like trees underwater and gray fish swimming between them. My hand creates ripples.

I think about drowning myself. The water cuts me. I decide against it. With all this pain, drowning might hurt too much.

`We bump up` against the beach of the island. The trees tower above us. I see the shacks ahead, the ones that used to be bars. I see no robots and I get chills. I didn't expect to see people? But I did expect to see those animatronic pirates. The fact that they're missing makes this whole place feel emptier.

Rowan chatters nervously and touches the trees as we walk. "The mirror Rowan went this way. Deeper and deeper into the center of it all. You know that ride they called The Center of the Moon or the Earth or whatever. And you spun around and around… Then they had this video that made you think you were flying and the whole place shook and shook and shook? Yeah like that. That's kind of how this is, but not? But anyway. Right. Come on, let's go let's go. I'm starting to remember things I don't want to remember and I don't like them. Shit. I feel so sick. We have to make this right? Don't you understand? We need to make this right?"

I stop. I can tell he doesn't remember any of it, not quite yet anyway. He doesn't remember murdering anyone, and I feel for him, I do. What a horrible thing to find out, that you're not the person you thought you were. That you've done horrible things, things you never even thought you would ever be capable of.

And yet, he has to know. And somehow, I have to be the one who tells him. I place my hand on his shoulder, and say with as much weight and seriousness as humanly possible. "You killed them all, you know. You said it was poetry."

He starts whimpering and wringing his hands and saying "No, no, no, no, no." He then starts rocking back and forth, faster and faster and faster. "No, no, no," over and over again, "No, no, no." Before I could stop him, he starts violently bashing his head against a tree.

I run forward, pull him back, push myself between him and the tree, holding him back. His forehead is bloody.

"I know, but the puppet did it. The puppets! I saw them all, in the mirror. All of the puppets. They had poetry carved in their bones. They did it! They did it! They used my face when they did it, but they did it! I could never have done that!"

I keep my hand on him, keep myself between him and the tree. I don't know what to believe anymore, I just know we need to stop this, we need to stop everything. "I know," I say, even though I don't know, not really. "I believe you."

And some part of me did believe him. After all I've seen, after all I've been through, a large part of me believed him.

"We need to make this right," he says with blood dripping into his eyes. He takes my arm and we move forward.

It hurts. Each step hurts. But we do it. We keep moving forward.

Brambles and thorns and hallways. Rambling corridors and emptiness and a sense of claustrophobia.

Rowan drones on and on about how it wasn't this bad before when he was a puppet or something like that. I find it odd that out of everything, the air here doesn't hurt me. The brambles don't cut. The vines are soothing to the touch. Like a slippery thing. Warm and inviting. The closer to the center of it all we go and there is a light emanating out. A strange golden light like a lamp in the darkness.

I hear the whispers of the dead around me. They talk about everyday things. Like they're still alive. Closer and closer we get. Closer and closer. Finally, the light is bright and beautiful and then our eyes adjust. And I'm in a small round room I've never seen before. The walls are covered in poetry. All sorts of verse and words and ramble-ons. Rowan is gone. I turn around to find him and he's gone. I don't even hear him anymore. All I can hear now are the whispers of ghosts.

All of the light comes from a giant crystal that towers over me in the center of the room. Golden salt crystals growing up and spiky. Torn from the ground and from the stone. Frozen inside like amber are butterflies. And in the center of this crystal is a woman without a face.

The space where her eyes, nose, and mouth should be is just skin.

If I look closely, I can see that skin is stitched over the face, skin from a back or a stomach or something else. She's naked and covered in cuts. Circular spiral cuts that flow over her body.

I hear Rowan babbling to himself, and realize he's reappeared on the floor behind me, rocking back and forth. I ignore him as I walk forward, the crystal summoning me. I feel its pull, like a magnet in my bones yanking me towards her. Rowan would have to take care of himself now.

I touch the crystal and I feel electrified. My hair stands on end.

This was his daughter. The Poet. The Poet the Alice girl was talking about, the same poet mentioned in the website Stacey showed me. One and the same, I recognize it in a way that defies all logic. I know it just by touch, my heart thunders this knowledge inside of me, telling me everything.

All the pain is gone now. I know that she was his daughter and he made her into his poetry and then used her. She is the gateway. She is the Dead Snake Tree brought into this world.

I look at her and I can see the shadow of the tree. The light. It is in the outline of the tree of my dreams.

How are all these things connected? Is the Poet here? Are any of us here? His ghost infects us. This tree is the center of it all. His daughter is the nucleus of it all. He made poetry of his own daughter and used it to escape, to bring in words from another spatial realm, something folded up, inside of our world like an origami universe shoved into the folds of time.

"What am I supposed to do?" I ask and there is no answer. "Tell me. What is it?"

The air is filled with lightning.

And I realize that I need help. I need so much help right now, and I know that there is only one person who could help me, who had the power to make this all right. Not Rowan, that's for certain, he's useless right now.

No, it's Stacey. I wonder if I could scratch a door with one of these rocks and it would work just the same? Maybe. I have to text her first, I have to let her know that I need her. That she has to draw the chalk door and connect it here, with me. To come and help me help them. To come and save the world.

I text her quickly, and don't even wait for her to respond. I run over to the blank wall behind the crystal and scavenge around for a loose white stone. It takes a few moments, the stone doesn't have to be perfect, just needs to cut an image of a door into the wall. There, there, I think I have it. There.

Nervous fingers, grasping the edges, everything is shaking and shimmers slightly. Fuck. Please get my text Stacey, please get it soon. I hear the phone bleep, notifying me of a text. I decide not to check it, but instead to start marking up the door. Wobbly, uneven, and it takes longer, it takes a lot of work to cram that rock onto the stone and make scratchy white image. But it works, yes, eventually it works.

I pause, looking at it for a brief second. I close my eyes; I count backwards from ten. My heart is pounding and my blood sounds like a river in my ears. And I hear a popping noise, and a muffled cry, as I open my eyes and see an arm stretch on through, then a head, and then...yes, yes...

Stacey? But… Oh fuck! She's covered in cuts and spirals and her face... Cuts around her cheeks and her eyes like someone was trying to cut her face off and failed.

What happened to her?

Tripping, I run over.

Her whole body drops, crying and bleeding.

I hold her. I don't speak; I just hold her. I know the work of a poet when I see it. I bite back the sobs and I'm breathless.

Eventually she talks.

"We need to burn the tree. The Poet has his hooks in everyone, has his poetry in everything. He has the ghosts now, too, and they power this dark engine of his art." She leans in closer to me, closer, her gaze deadly serious. "We're all a part of it, understand? All of us manipulated by him for this sole purpose. To bring the undying horrors from beyond the edges of our world here, and make them real." Her eyes widen in terror. "Oh Hazel, they are so horrible. I don't even know what to call them. Alien creatures? Monsters? Gods? I don't know. But, the Poet hates the world, and he wishes to feed it to them in his madness."

This feels like too much to take in, that my whole concept of the world is breaking before my very eyes. And yet, everything I've seen until now, everything that happened up until this exact moment, feels like it's leading right towards this truth. That reality itself is a shadow, and that all sorts of impossible things bubble around the edges. My stomach twisting about, my mind reeling. I'm dizzy and sick and could barely think, but I have to, I have to think, I have work to do, I need to stop reality from breaking even more. But none of it, none of it makes sense. And yet, all of it makes sense. My head throbs with the impossible contradiction, and I had to stifle the urge to laugh. That's what crazy people do in moments like this, laugh.

"And destroying the tree will stop him? How?" I'm not sure I want to know the answer to this.

"The tree gets rid of the ghosts. All of them will be gone. They will stop powering his poetry, stop summoning the horrible things from beyond time to devour us all."

From the brambles behind us, I can still her Rowan jabbering. Now he's repeating some of what she said. He's completely gone now. His mind elsewhere.

I can still feel Clara next to me and all those other ghosts I've accumulated over the years. All of my memories walking around, talking to each other. I can sense them, like they are songs, liquid things like water or fire or shadows. Things you can fill up other things with. I can't say goodbye to them, can I? I don't want to say goodbye to them.

It would be too easy to say goodbye.

And even this memory. Yes, this. Maybe this will be gone too.

Allison at the Safe House. She was there before we got there, maybe for a year. The one who introduced me and Stacey who I try not to think about, but she's always here next to me. Like all the other ghosts, always here, always talking to me as I drift off to sleep. She was the thinnest and needed a wheel chair to move. They fed her through a tube in her stomach. She was a veteran of pain, a survivor of all those teen angst years.

She was stronger than anyone else. The nurses, the doctors, the therapists… No one could reach her. Not her parents, no one. They were sad all the time when around her and they couldn't penetrate her shell. They couldn't make her be the little girl they wanted her to be. The kind of girl they wanted us all to be. One without pain. One without misery. A doll they could dress up in pretty doll clothes and take to the prom and marry or whatever.

But no.

Not Allison. She was power in a chair. She was full of needle pokes and starvation. She cut and it was more than a cut. It was bone deep. She wanted to dig her bones out from her skin. She was the one who showed us all that Safe House wasn't that safe at all. They couldn't protect us. They couldn't save us from ourselves. No matter how many times they promised.

She threw herself down the steps from her wheelchair three months after I came to Safe House. They found her body crumpled up on the bottom of the stairs. They tried to get us out and away but too late.

We already spied it. We already knew what she was trying to say. There is no such thing as a safe house. Or a safe life. Or a safe anything.

"Even Allison?" I say. I know what this will do to Stacey, but I say it anyway. She's holding her head now, like she's trying to keep her face glued on her skull.

"Don't say that, like...don't. You have no right."

"We will lose Allison. Won't we? We will lose her."

Stacey's voice is now small. "I..I.. Ugh. Don't start that! You can't make this about her. Fuck. Stop it. Okay?"

The lightning in the air is now in our lungs. We breathe the electricity in. It fills us with all those sparks. The lightning. The fire. The fire inside of me. I breathe in deeper and feel like my heart is a Tesla coil.

"We might not have to do that."

She looks at me. Blood on either side of her cheeks. "Do what?"

"Close the door. There might be another way."

Stacey looks at me. "Okay." She says. "Okay."

She collapses, twitching. Her face slides off. I call out, "Rowan! I know how you can redeem yourself. I need you to take someone to the hospital."

I lean over through the brambles and I see him in a shadowed corner with his knees up to his chest. He's rocking back and forth and talking to himself. The words aren't clear, clean words. They are confused, broken. Words of someone else's poetry.

Oh shit. The Poet is trying to possess him, too.

"Rowan!" I shout.

He turns and looks at me, snapping back into it for a brief moment. "The hospital?" he asks.

"Yes. She's right over there. You need to hurry the fuck up. Maybe even call an ambulance? Save her! It doesn't make everything all right, but you will have done one thing right. If you save one person, you save the world or some shit like that."

"I guess?"

"Just fucking do it."

He crawls through the thorns, branches expanding trying to stop him. He goes on anyway, even with thorns ripping up clothes and tearing at his skin, leaving it raw and angry and bleeding. He moves out and into the room of the crystal daughter. He doesn't even seem to see her. Maybe he knows what was in here already. He approaches Stacey both in awe and shock and horror all at once.

"Go on," I say, "Call an ambulance to meet you out there. I have something I need to do. I trust you on this, okay?"

He says okay. And then I walk through the chalk door.

I don't know what to expect on the other side. My fingers push through and I feel water. I shove my hand through, arm through, and then head through. I close my mouth. I want to keep this renewed lightning in my heart. I don't want the flames under my skin to be put out again.

I swim and I don't know where I'm going. The water is warm and blue. I don't see anything else, no fish or weeds or other life… I keep my mouth closed as I swim.

How do I travel here? Stacey made climbing through the chalkboard doors look so easy.

I hope she's okay. I can't lose another friend. I can't do it. Fuck. Can't. Fuck. Hell.

I push forward. I remember my dreams of drowned cities and bodies asleep floating like planks, suspended in the water. Not going up or down… Is this where I dream? Where I go when I dream?

…and then my hand moves through. I feel air and I feel like I'm real again. Maybe I was make-believe before, a thought waiting to become real.

Then it's my elbow and then the other hand and then head, neck, and shoulders and I fall out. I'm not wet at all but I'm gasping for air.

I stand up and I look around and I see that I'm here again… Back to the old ruin of a school where Clara and I used to go and drink and dream of the Dead Snake Tree...

I fell through the spray-painted body that extends several walls and halls. I bend over and vomit up waves. They splash against the ground, and sound like the lake. Fish in my lungs, in my throat and up they come squirming and wiggling. The gray fish slide between my teeth. They fall out of my mouth and flop in the water.

How did that happen? I thought I'd kept my mouth shut?

I breathe. Inhale. Exhale. I feel it still in my chest. That lightning singing. It did not get weaker with water. Instead, it got stronger. I feel it now sparking, lighting up my insides.

Okay. I'm okay now. Okay. I'm okay now.

I stand, propped up against the wall. The room stands still. Every part of me aches like when I had the flu.

I need to find Clara's mom. I need to find the Susans. I know this now. I need to find them and I need to make sure that the Poet isn't still infecting them, that we were really able to stop him once and for all. Else, it could all happen all over again.

But how the fuck do I find Clara's mom? I should leave here. I should? I should. But first. Fuck. I can't believe I'm doing this but I have to do this. I feel like it's important.

FUCK I MISS HER LIKE FUCK FUCK

Of course. Of course they are here. I can see down to the end of the hallway I'm in. I hide behind collapsed parts of the wall and have vines across my face. I peek out from behind the leaves. It's like all of this is folding together: my life was origami. Or maybe it is that fucking Poet. Maybe this is all some way of moving us like chess pieces?

And there they were. The Susans. Clara's mom. There they were in the garden where Clara and I used to go and drink.

The tree dances in the center, its leaves flowing around them. Clara's mom is in the center of it all. Her head is down. She sits. She is naked. She has cuts on her. Spirals and symbols. Her right hand is raised to the sun. Around her, in a circle, the Susans float in the air on fire. They are still, their hair hovering around them, their white eyes staring ahead at nothing. They have nothing else. Just pale emptiness for eyes.

The fire is red and orange and blue. It licks them and licks the air, flowing out from their heart. The fire: the heart all of it.

I should have a plan. I don't have a plan. This scene looks like a painting. I want to ask them if they are haunted by painters now and no longer infected with the ghost of a poet.

I suck in a deep breath, my lightning growing stronger as I hold my lungs still. Everything is full of fire.

I stand up. The vines fall from around me. The debris no longer hiding me.

I am solid. I am human. I am not infected with anything. I control the lightning. I am the fire that burns in my veins. I no longer want to cut myself out. I no longer want to remove this skin. I no longer want to burn everything to the ground. I embrace my lightning. I embrace my fire.

They don't see me. Are they blind? Like the little Alice girl with Rowan earlier. I wonder if they can't see like she couldn't see.

I take slow steps. I don't want to rush them. Rushing them would make everything explode inside of me and I want to keep this lightning calm as it burns up through my body. I feel alive.

Clara's dead and Stacey might be dead. But then again, all these ghosts who follow me everywhere will stay with me. I can stop all of this and fix all of this and keep my ghosts.

I love my ghosts.

I walk closer now and they don't move at all. I feel like the pit of my stomach is falling out of me. Something is wrong about all of this. Something can't be right I'm moving forward and I can't stop myself anymore. I need to end this. Will this end it? Will this kill off the poetry virus or will this only stop it from breathing for a moment? Later, will it exhale? Will the whole world become an epic poem?

That doesn't make sense.

I walk closer, each step longer than the last towards infinity. Each step a step of infinite numbers. I can't reach the end of any of this. I walk. I walk. And now? Now I stand at the entrance to the garden looking at the Susans on fire.

I remember that fire. That fire inside of the Susans. It was a fire of pain and depression and misery. It was a fire of divorce. Of a dad that never called or stopped in. A fire of a mom screaming in the dark each night and then sobbing alone. A fire of us losing a house. A fire of homeless hours. A fire constructed out of living in a car. And then a tent. And then searching for a work. A fire made of Safe House hours and trying not to cut myself. A fire of wanting to be sick. A fire that shows how sick I felt on the inside outside of my body. A fire of wanting to be healed. Of wanting to be made whole. A fire of waiting for the end of the world. Of waiting for absolution. A fire of waiting for freedom from yourself. A fire built on the freedom of skinless self. No longer body built of flesh. Just bone and blood and fire. A fire that wanted to get out and destroy… *Destroy* the fucking world.

I see them with my old fire.

And I think. No.

No. They can keep it. I have embraced my lightning.

Fuck them.

And then…

Clara's mom lifts her head up and looks at me and I gasp.

It is Clara's mom, not Clara. I have to keep telling myself that. She wears Clara's face. She has it stitched over her own. It looks leathery and preserved. The eye holes revealing eyes beneath them. This isn't Clara. This is Clara's mom still. I walk closer and she doesn't do anything. She just looks at me with those eyes behind the eyes.

I want to tear that face from her face. That's not her face; it's Clara's and she doesn't...she doesn't get to wear that. She doesn't. She can't.

I walk past the floating bodies of Susans. As I pass them their fire is extinguished like a candle flame snuffed out—whoosh. Their bodies crumple to the ground. As if, somehow, my very presence makes that fire go away. It's odd how calm the lightning makes me. I control it. I am in control of it.

Once the bodies hit the ground, the Susans try and stand up. Weak-armed, moving. Weak head tilting. Weak everything. Trying to move. But they give up. I see their faces change into fox faces, their body morph into fox bodies. They run off, some limping, some bounding, off into the building around us. The fire is gone out of them and now they are foxes. That seems right somehow.

I walk forward. It's just me and Clara's mom. She looks at me with curious eyes behind the skin mask. Did she try and do the same to Stacey? Was that why Stacey's face was like that?

"Bring her back. Bring her back. I just want to bring her back. What did I do? What have I done? I'm not myself anymore. I'm not anyone anymore. What happened to me?"

Clara comes out. From behind the tree. I know she's a ghost because her body is translucent and blue like water like waves.

I want to run over and hug her but I stop. I just watch. This isn't about me. This is about bonds that burn us alive from the inside out.

I watch her walk over. I watch her take her face from her mom's face. I watch her throw it to the ground. Her mom's face is slick with blood. Daughter blood? Clara's blood.

The ghost doesn't seem to care. Instead? She stands her mom up and they embrace.

I wonder what being a ghost is like.

This is their moment. Even though I want to hug Clara and talk to her, have an all-night conversation where we sit and drink. I would like that. Drink and talk and be just like we were. At the start of all this. Before all of this.

But they need this. This is their moment.

So, I turn. I walk into the shadows of the ruins around me.

Allison's ghost is like how she saw herself. Sick is what she saw. Always sick on the inside. Pain inside. Wanting that pain outside.

That's the thing most people don't understand about depression. It fucking hurts. Most people don't see it. They look at you and they see normal. We want our pain and sick on the outside so they can see it and maybe understand us.

Allison was like that so much. She starved herself and they had to feed her through a tube in her stomach, so frail from malnutrition they had her in a wheelchair. They had to pick up her little body, her sack of bones tied with flesh body and lay her in bed.

When they found her dead, we all sat in circles and watched. They yelled at us, scattered us like birds. But when they weren't looking, we would come back. We drew chalk circles where her body had been. Marking it. Always marking it. They would wash it away and the next morning, it would be there again. Again and again. Made with different color chalk each time.

Her ghost looks like that now. Body crumpled and weak. Still a tube out of her stomach and leading to a bag hung by a metal pole. Her eyes are shadows, her skin like vellum. You could see through it to the blue veins underneath it all.

We all admired her. We saw courage in her darkness. It was why I cut. It was why Stacey ate those inedible things. Because it hurt. It always hurt all the time. And they would all look at us with either pity or hatred. They couldn't understand. They couldn't see that this was how we survived. Day in day out, this was how we survived.

I'm in the ocean between doors and Allison's ghost is beside me leading me through all of it. Taking me through everything. She knows something I don't and she wants to tell me. But her mouth is too weak; her teeth are like chalk. She can't speak without squeaking in pain.

I know that this can't be it yet. The Poet wasn't there at the Dead Snake Tree. The Poet is still out there, moving through bodies, infecting those around. I need to stop the virus.

Allison looks like she wants me to close the door, to burn the Dead Snake Tree. But I won't do that. I can't do that. I need her and I need Clara. I need my ghosts. So, fuck it. I'll figure something else out. I'll make this right in other ways. There must be other ways. There are always other ways.

She's too weak to go through the chalk door and the other side and so I go by myself. She flickers in that vast ocean between doors almost real and then she's not. I want to grab her and hold her and make her permanent again. Maybe if it was a different life, she would've found her own lightning in her heart and maybe death wouldn't be the answer.

Oh fuck. Oh fuck. I didn't expect that.
To see...
Oh fuck!
Oh, goddamn it.

Stacey's face is sewn on. I see small bits of dried blood around the stitches and it looks like it might slide again but it stops.

I want to close the chalk door but I know this is it. I have to do this but it hurts so much to see this. To see Stacey like this.

Her face is always in motion, always about ready to slide off. There are spirals cut into her cheeks and her forehead, primal symbols like sigils. Like rituals. I see them all over her body. Some patches of her skin gone. Stripped off. On her hands. On her arms.

I should've stayed and called an ambulance. I should've done what Stacey had said originally. I shouldn't have been so connected to these ghosts.

Her teeth look wrong. Her fingers look wrong. She's sitting there, waiting for me. Waiting. In front of the girl in crystal waiting. I see the girl in crystal, her eyes watching me from behind the skin mask.

Had I been manipulated by the Poet this whole time? Had the virus planned it all out? Was this it, would he escape again?

I walk out and I feel like pain everywhere again, pain because my trust was burned away. The lightning inside soothes that pain a little, feeds on it. I feel myself become stronger and stronger and stronger and stronger and stronger and stronger...

She's putting on a show for me, just me.

This is not how I want to see her. This is not how I want to see Rowan.

I walk forward. My legs wobble. What the fuck. I guess I see it. I guess I see all of this and I want to stop seeing this. I need to stop this. It can't happen again. Again and again and I can't.

I know Rowan wasn't a saint. He did bad things but still... I remember who he was before the poetry took over and this didn't need to happen.

"What did you do?" I say as I walk.

And I know Stacey isn't Stacey anymore. She can't be Stacey anymore. Stacey's eyes are different...wrong. They're like the poet's eyes. Had he possessed her? Had he possessed Stacey?

"I wrote a pretty poem on the bones of this boy."

I close my eyes. I know my hair is standing up because the electricity is burning through me now. I don't want her to be infected.

Maybe burning out the Dead Snake Tree is the only way to get everything to normal again. No more dreams like those dreams. No more poetry infections. No more ghosts and no more chalk doors.

Poetry is a ritual. Serial killers have rituals. When we were at the Safe House, we traded rituals. Our rituals were how we controlled our environment, ourselves…

Cutting is a ritual. Graduating is a ritual. Time moving is a ritual of planets and gravity. Our movements through space itself are a ritual. Our mornings are rituals of waking; our nights rituals of sleep. Rituals are agents of change that make us different. make us what we want to become.

We perform that ritual that moves us out of the state of becoming to the actual thing. Poetry is about becoming this thing we want to be, becoming these rituals, pushing us into what we want to become. Serial killers want to become something monstrous. It's about power over the environment. Rituals provide us that control. We control what we become and it's all about moving past the liminal moments. Who we are, when we are on the other side… All these rituals are doorways of transformation.

The poetry of Rowan's body:

Fingers are bent far back and his head is dangling down. I think his ears are cut off and replaced with honeycombs filled with still living bees, honey dripping down his cheeks. His eyes are gray things, his mouth broken apart. All the teeth are gone, placed on the ground in a circle around him.

Circles. Circles are part of all rituals. This shape is the key shape. It is the key of everything. Circles are keys.

His clothes are gone and his stomach is cut in such a way that his organs fall out of his body like a waterfall of viscera. In his stomach are more bees.

And then I see his head move. And his mouth twitches and he's alive still. Just barely but alive still.

I quiver. What. *What.*

It's not just some abstract death now. It's dying. It's the liminal moment between life and death. The ritual must not be complete; the transformation must not be complete yet. Maybe me coming, me seeing this was all a part of this. It had to be me. Me seeing this. This was the becoming. The transformation.

I like the liminal moments. I like not knowing who I am. I like being in the middle of the transformation. I like it when everything is changing and that feeling that everything is different now. That the whole world moves and is alive with that motion. I love that.

I don't like the finished transformation. I love the spark before the fire. I love the smell in the air before it rains. I love the feeling of sinking down in water before drowning but not drowning. To become an actuality is to kill off all possibilities. And that was one thing I had over the Poet. That was one thing I had over this virus. I loved the moments between. I lived in those crevices of our world. I loved them.

The poet was addicted to transformation and I was addicted to the possibility of being and not being. I was addicted to the chrysalis. He wanted butterflies. I was never going to give him that.

Rowan didn't deserve this. Even though all the horrors he's created...he was infected. Then again, does that absolve him?

Still. *This.* I don't want any more of this. This needs to stop.

Stacey stands right in front of the white chalk door, laughs. "You won't kill her. You won't kill her. This body is so perfect for now. Oh, did she really think that this is the ends of ends? No! No! I am the words and the fire and the light. I am the patterns of stars and I will become what I need and what I want. I will transcend it. My poetry is about that! That is it! But no, no, nothing ever seems right, nothing seems to work. This is all wrong, always wrong..."

Stacey leans in, leans closer. Her eyes wide and frantic, her hands on either side of my face. I feel like I'm trapped, that everything has come around full circle again and I just want to run away and be done with all this.

"Let me do it to you. Let me help you transcend it all and become a poem. I know you want to. I heard your conversation with Rowan, I did. You want this transformation. You want to burn and burn and then come out ghost and all. I can see it in your eyes..."

And Stacey's face brightens all the more, she's hypnotized me completely, I want to pull away, I need to pull away. But I can't pull away, I'm completely sucked in. The poet, that's the poet in her voice, and it's all liquid honey, pouring into my thoughts. Her eyes are everything I see now, bright and like two gold coins, flickering and moving back and forth, back and forth, back and forth. I feel like his words are my thoughts now, and I can't tell them apart anymore. All I feel is this need, this need for transformation, transfiguration. Ascendance, yes, to become something new and monstrous and beautiful all at once. I need it so badly I can taste it, and the very promise of it is like wine on my lips, in my gut, my thoughts growing dim and fuzzy with the need for change, to burn away the old and become new.

"All your friends are dead and even Stacey here? She'll be dead soon. I can't stick around sin this. The rituals aren't right if I use the same form, the same fingers, the same flesh. So, come on. Become something. Become a ghost. Let me use this poetry to transform you. Let that skin slide off all slick and become the ghost you know you have inside of you."

Rowan opens his mouth and it looks like he wants to scream but instead bees crawl out. His eyes panic. His mouth twitches. Now he's crying he's just… He's crying.

Fucking hell. I can't watch this I can't. I can't do this. I can't. I need to stop this. I can't.

"Kill him," Stacey says. "Kill him. It's the first step. I know you have it in you. What you did to Dylan? That was so beautiful. Now, do it to a living boy. Finish this poem, make that ritual complete. And then? Oh. Then the poetry will transform you. Oh. Yes. Make him a ghost, and then, you'll make yourself a ghost. You will be mirrors of transformation. I know it. You know it. Do it."

Stacey leans back, away from me, moves her hands from my face, smiling. She reaches down and pulls out a bloodied hunting knife from her belt, holding it up to me so I can see it in great detail. There are bits of skin on it, and it makes me shiver. "Do it. Make him a ghost."

His eyes roll back in his head and he makes noises with his mouth like a kitten mewling. More bees crawl out and buzz around his head.

I move forward. Should I do it? He is in so much pain. I look at Stacey. She is in so much pain. I could take her knife.

She sees me thinking and her face slides a little when she tries to smile. "All this pain is temporary. All pain is a part of our poetry, part of all art. There is no transformation without pain. The ritual demands it. The poetry demands it. It is our price for moving on and becoming something greater than ourselves. Help him. Push him. Finish the poem. Complete the circle."

I remember Stacey and me running through the halls of Safe House and laughing. It's hard to forget these moments. Those days when everything was calm and real. We had happiness in those moments. Outside, it was raining and we heard it hit the windows. All of the lights flickered with the sound of thunder. We knew we should be in our rooms getting ready for group therapy, talking in a circle and everything. Share all of that, share all of this.

But in that moment right then, we ran. We know they'd look for us soon. But we ran.

Stacey knew a place we could hide. They found Allison's body that morning and so they were extra harsh about us stepping out. In our sadness, they only saw more pain, pain they felt they had to stop. All of the time, like it was their job to keep us happy. If we felt sad, they strapped us in and tried to control us, tried to make us follow their little rules. They forced a new ritual on us, an external ritual, one they felt like we couldn't control.

Allison found a way to control them and they had hated it. The ritual they imposed on her fell off and she just laughed at it. She kept her own secrets and kept her own rituals. And what she transformed into was death and I guess death was the strongest ritual we had: the last transformation.

She was dead and we didn't see any purpose in following their rituals, their rules. So, we ran. Ran to the hidden places. These were cracks in the old mansion. The halls they didn't want us to know about. The bookcase that swung away and revealed long old forgotten wine cellars. It was like a bad Gothic novel, all of these hidden places.

We moved into them. We became cracks of the house. We lived in the secret places. We talked only in whispers. We didn't want to finish the ritual: our ritual, any of their rituals or even Allison's rituals.

Later, we would get reprimanded and punished and spend times in solitary rooms that smelled of spiders and dust and mildew. But it was worth it. And every moment we got, we sneaked away and broke the ritual of where to be and who to be. And we created that chalk outline again on the floor where Allison died. We all had hidden stashes of chalk. We made sure she was remembered always…always. As one who created her own transformations. As one who would not succumb to the rituals of others.

And here Stacey is, letting someone else's rituals control her, control her life. And it wants to control me. That fucking Poet. That motherfucker. He wants to control me like he controlled Clara's mom and Clara. Like he controlled Rowan and all of his poet friends.

Like he controlled his own daughter there frozen and now a gateway between worlds.

Fuck him. Fuck his shitty poetry.

I knock the knife out of her hand, watch it scatter.

"Fuck *you*."

Stacey's face slides almost all the way down.

And I say, "Your poetry sucks."

Rowan twitches.

"Critics are so passé," she says. "I don't care what you think about any of this. The only point of the ritual is the changes we create. Not the way some simpleton views it. But how those changes erupt inside of us. Making us different people. Burning people burning brightly. I brought all of you so many gifts through the years!"

And as Stacey speaks, Rowan collapses in his circle of teeth. His head bursts when Stacey kicks it. The bees are angry and hovering. I hear them buzz in a fog around us.

I close my eyes. The lightning glows and grows. I can control this. I am it. I am everything. I will not kill her. I cannot kill Stacey. But I can see the Poet in the air hovering, a ghost controlling her like a puppet. He is mostly translucent, flickering, like some old black and white movie reel we watched in history class. His face looks unreal, like a ghostly mask made of skin sewn together, and his hands are in the air, moving like marionette hands, controlling her.

I don't want to do this. I want my ghosts. I need my ghosts.

But fuck, I have to stop this… I have stop it all and I need to do this.

Goodbye Clara and Rowan and Dylan and fuck. All those girls from our Safe House and Allison. Especially Allison. I will miss all of them all of them oh, all of them. Fucking hell. I don't want to do this. Fucking hell.

I open my eyes.

And I let my lightning sing.

The crystal shatters with my song. And the little daughter crumples out, her body falling apart like a broken toy as each body part falls off. No blood. None of that. No gore. The crystal falls.

The poet screams silently, his face burning up, his body turning to fog and light and then to nothingness. As Stacey collapses, twitching and sick and all of those wounds and her face and…

Oh fuck.

I want to save her. Just one person. I need to save one fucking person.

I pull out my phone and I dial 911 and I hold my breath. I feel everything holding its breath: the island, the lake, Rowan's bees… All of it holding its breath and waiting. The whole world inhaling and living in its lungs. Wishing good luck on trapped air. We need that luck. We do.

33

They take us away in separate ambulances. The lights of sirens whirl around us. I've never felt like this before. Not empty. Not on fire. No lightning. Nothing. Just me. I am me. I am just me or something and now that's okay.

I long to reach out to Stacey. To see how she's doing. To see if she's going to the same hospital as I am. I have so many questions, but I can't move, I can't call her.

I don't remember much. But I think surgery? I think. I know they gave me blood. I'm full of someone else's blood. And I have a room. For a while, I was breathing through a mask. Now, I'm hooked up to some machines. There are bags. And I'm all stitched up. I realize all that cutting. They fixed all that cutting. Was it my cutting? I don't know. I look down.

Some of the cuts are in spirals. I don't remember doing that? Maybe I did. Regardless, I feel whole now.

They said that I opened up my stomach? I don't remember doing any of that. I just remember calling the ambulance for Stacey and Rowan. They couldn't save him. It's hard to save someone filled with bees.

I laugh now. I guess they have me on some strange stuff to kill the pain. Maybe that's something I've needed for so long. Something to kill the pain?

Or maybe I just need to embrace it. Yay pain.

My brother's sitting over my bed. I see him there on the edge and he says "hi." It seems so strange now. Everything we've been through and all of that. "I guess it's all over now, isn't it?" he asks.

And I smile what I think is a good smile and say, "Yeah."

"I had this dream last night where the tree was on fire. You know? The Dead Snake Tree. It was on fire. And the fire was silver. It was weird, right? I mean. Weird." He looks right through me, "What did you do, Hazel? What did you do?"

"I fixed everything?"

He pats on my leg. "I guess so."

We sit there and stare into space for a bit. We're both survivors now and I guess that brings us closer in some ways and pushes us apart in other ways. We're so different, like two completely new people. I didn't save him; I didn't set him free. But maybe I stopped all of this.

It's lonely now. The ghosts all gone. I feel all of this emptiness around me. I'm so dull on the inside. Not depressed but not alive either, like some sort of half-life. A life waiting to move on. Or maybe a life that moved on. I don't know. Maybe this is what a survivor feels like. Maybe.

Mom comes by and even Dad with his awkward attempts at good Dad. Mom is sad and happy at once. I wonder when she's going to get a break, when will her life be some normal boring life that she wants to escape from? I want to give her that life.

Later, I'm off the pain meds and my brother is there sitting next to me. I think about Clara's ghost and how I miss her. I miss talking to her all night over a jug of shitty wine.

And now I'm talking with my brother and it feels the same. Those same kind of epic conversations me and Clara used to have together.

"Do you ever feel guilty?" he asks.

"About?"

A beat in his words. A thought, I reach over and our hands touch.

"Surviving. You know? Like. Every day I feel guilty. Like I should be dead."

I don't respond. I know what he's talking about. I feel the same way. "I feel guilty for not doing it sooner? I don't know. It got out of control and now...now it's all gone from us."

"The air feels empty. You know? Like there was something there, and now it's gone."

"Empty."

"Yeah. Um. Like...before the air was water. And now it's not."

I don't say anything. I think I know what he means. Before the air was filled with ghosts. And now all the ghosts are gone.

"Yeah. I know. I guess."

"Right."

And then I have to ask because no one's said anything yet. "How's Stacey? You know, the girl I came in with. Do you know? Do you know if she's okay?"

He shrugs and says, "No, I don't know. I guess. I don't know. Why?"

"She's an old friend. A really old friend."

We watch the car lights like halos outside of the windows for a bit and we try and shrug off these feelings. All of these fucking feelings. I want to feel better, like everything is better. I want it all to be right now. That's what I went through, you know? To make everything right. But it's not. I don't think it will ever be all the way right.

Stacey is in a wheelchair. She pushes it up to my bed. I don't know why I'm bedridden and she's not. All of the cuts on her face are stitched up but she seems fine. Face-wise anyway. She's got this oxygen thing under her nose and her hands are bandaged.

She reminds me of Allison. She even has a tube in her stomach leading out to some bag she's connected to. And I want to say that. I want to tell her she looks like our old friend. But I don't know if that's the right thing to do anymore? At least not now.

A part of me wonders if she was present during those moments when she was infected with poetry, when she wanted me to kill Rowan, or when she did what she did to Rowan, or when she asked me to finish him. Does she remember that? How does she feel about having that inside of her? Do I dare ask her?

I can't tell by just looking at her. I want to be able to see if she remembers what I remember. If she was like what Rowan was: a puppet or a mirror watching outside of her body. But her eyes don't betray her.

I wonder if it's like some infections when the virus hangs out in your blood, dead, but still there. Like the virus becomes a part of you. I wonder if that's it. If she is filled with dead poetry.

She comes a little closer. It sounds like it's hard for her to speak.

"Thanks," she says.

"Yeah. No problem?"

"No, really, like thank you a million times over. Thanks."

"Okay."

"Yeah, okay."

A moment of silence between us. "I think, you know. I think we did it. It's like, done and that's it."

She nods and I think it hurts.

"Yeah. The air feels different."

"Casper said that. It is different. We did something. Like we changed the whole world on a cellular level or something? I don't know."

"I guess."

And more silence. She leans over; her hand touches mine. I grasp it. It feels frail in my fingers, like my brother's hands when he was in the coma. Part of me wants to be in a coma for a little while, just to take a break. Just to rest.

"I feel so exhausted all the time right now. Not like, emptied out or anything. Just really fucking tired."

"At least you don't have to worry about your face and shit."

And I laugh a little, like the kind of laugh you make when you know you're expected to laugh at something.

"I guess, yeah. I guess I'm lucky or something."

Stacey sits back, looks up at the ceiling. "How much longer do you think we'll be here?"

"I don't know." And I don't, I don't really know. Nor do I want to know. For the first time in a long time, I feel safe, in a way I haven't since I was tiny and we had a stable home and family.

And Stacey smiles, and when she does her face crinkles a bit, looks loose. Like it's barely on, and I feel this overwhelming sadness. Not matter how much the stitch us together or fix us, we will be forever changed.

She speaks hesitatingly between her teeth, and I wonder if the smile is painful for her or not. "Let's do something stupid."

"Like what?"

"Like, um. I don't know. Let's watch old sitcoms on my tablet."

I laugh. I can't help myself, even though it hurts like hell to laugh. Every one of my stitches scream. "Okay. Yeah that sounds stupid."

"Right? But like all this seriousness, all of this death and everything. Maybe we need to be stupid. Maybe we need to do something stupid."

"Right. I guess."

"Come on. We need to forget ourselves for a little bit. Just a tiny bit."

And I nod, and feel the weight of everything against us. All of our experiences until now pushing against us. It feels so heavy, and I sigh. "Stacey?"

"Yeah?"

"I really miss Allison's ghost."

"I know. I miss all of them."

Instead of watching sitcoms, we go to her Dropbox folder and she has pictures I didn't know about. Pictures of us at Safe House. I don't even know how she got them. Even Allison is there. And she looks so different than I remembered her. She didn't look strong or sick. She just looks so lost and lonely and haunted.

And then I look at us, all of us and I realize we all looked like that. We all looked so different than I remembered. I remember every one of us as a proud warrior, wielding our personal rituals like shields against the onslaught of time.

But that's not it. We look like waifs and shadows and we look so broken and lost. It hurts my heart to see the truth in all of us. But there we were.

Flip, flip, flip.

There we were.

Survivors.

ACKNOWLEDGEMENTS

I would like to give thanks to Darin Bradley, Robert S. Wilson, Natania Barron, Michelle Muenzler, and Jonathan Wood for reading it over as I wrote it and giving me killer notes.

Also like to thank my editor, Katherine Silva, for helping me edit this into fighting shape and plucking it out of the slush and giving it a home. Also, special thanks to Third Estate Books for taking a risk and publishing this weird little novel.

Also thanks to Victoria Dovensky for being awesome and supporting me in tons of different ways, and my kids Ashlyn and Liam Jessup, for putting up with my odd hours of writing weird horror novels, and then listening to the plots in my own rambling ways.

Special thanks to my mom and dad for supporting me even though I wrote icky gross horror novels.

Thanks also to Werner Books, for always supporting local authors (including yours truly) and being the best bookstore in Erie, PA.

TRIGGER WARNINGS

SUICIDEMUSIC contains blood, gore, depression, self-harm, suicidal ideology, depictions of homelessness, death, burning, insects, animal death, decapitation, trauma, grief, drowning, and harm to birds.

If you or a loved one is facing any mental health issues just know you're not alone, and if you need help you can always call the Suicide and Crisis Lifeline at 988.

THE MONOLOGIST
by Aquino Loayza

What's life without risk?

At least that's what Patrick Gallagher tells himself as he arrives in Las Vegas at the peak of the Cold War with a dream that can't be bought in gold or jewels: To become a standup comedian, a monologist. But nobody can run away from their past, no matter how bright their future may seem. The world isn't as clear as it appears. Will Patrick succeed? Or will he discover that everything has its price and some costs can't be quantified in a dollar bill?

In this queer revolutionary imagining of 1963 Las Vegas, Aquino Loayza, Author of the Queer Cosmic Epic: Deep, explores the seedy underbelly of Sin City in its infancy as Patrick Gallagher embarks on his quest to defy the odds and become The Monologist.

BURY MY HEART WITH A KEYBOARD
by Jacy Morris

Jacy Morris' collection is an assault on Indigenous identity and stereotypes, an exploration of what it means to be Indigenous in a world where identity is commercialized and weaponized. 13 stories of the past, present, and future, all exploring different aspects of our world. At times brutal, at times hauntingly nostalgic, Bury My Heart with a Keyboard refuses to pull punches and revels in its gruesome truths. Filled with callous gods, broken souls, and a constant rejection of the status quo, Bury My Heart with a Keyboard is all you can handle and more.

BLACK OUT THE STARS
by Christopher Bond

Marcus, a man estranged from his family, returns to his roots amid a backdrop of generational trauma in rural, poverty-stricken Ohio, only to find that not all family secrets die given time. As Marcus helps his uncle drain a pond on their ancestral property, he uncovers the dark secrets of his family and the land they've called home.

"Christopher Bond has crafted a pond scum gothic that reeks of ghosts and regret. Hold your breath before diving into *BLACK OUT THE STARS*. It might be your last." - Clay McLeod Chapman, author of *WAKE UP AND OPEN YOUR EYES*

Paul Jessup is a critically acclaimed, award winning writer of spooky stuff. Active pro member of HWA, he's had publications in countless magazines over the years, including Nightmare, Apex Magazine, Clarkesworld, PostScripts, Interzone, Psuedopod, and tons more. His short stories have been honorable mentions in many Year's Best collections, including Best Horror of the Year, Year's Best Horror and Fantasy, and Best Science Fiction of the Year. In 2000 he won the Virginia Perryman award for excellence in short fiction, and in 2022 his short story (Skinless Man Counts to Five) was listed on the Recommended Reading List for the Stoker Awards.

He has lots of novels and short story collections published, mostly in the small press. His latest books are Glass House (a haunted house novel), Skinless Man Counts to Five and Other Tales of the Macabre (a short story collection), and Daughter of the Wormwood Star (a horror novel about a satanic cult). He has been published and translated in many different countries, including England, Ireland, Poland and Japan.

* 9 7 9 8 2 1 8 6 9 7 6 2 4 *